# RED BLOOD, WHITE OX

Lisa R. Bush

*To Lucas and Kenzie, my constant source of inspiration.*

*To Terri, my best friend and greatest support, and Carol, my designated coach, thank you.*

# INTRODUCTION

Before North versus South, it was Akers versus Caudill in a deadly war between families in Clay County, Kentucky. "Red Blood, White Ox" takes place in 1849, just a few years before the Civil War. Despite her parents' warnings about marrying into the feud, Matilda Abner says yes to Billy Akers, their short marriage, full of hope, was littered with violence and injustice.

The story begins with Matilda lying on her death bed, riddled with guilt and haunted by the memories of her past. Before she leaves this world she must repent and confess to her husband, Ira, the tragic love story of her and her beloved, Billy. She must relive the violent attack that left her brutalized, the devotion of her then-husband who is determined to protect her, and the tragedy that ends their marriage. The story takes you to a time when life and the law were much simpler, yet easily tainted. The Baker clan held great power in the mountains of Clay County, but within that power was a curse. You will have a front-row seat from crime to court case to tragic conclusion, all nestled in a small eastern Kentucky town.

This fictional story is inspired by actual events that occured in the life of my great-great-grandmother, Matilda. During my research, I was struck by the lack of information regarding Matilda's side of the story. There were many rumors and folklore, but little was known about her. Billy, on the other hand, was a member of the powerful Baker (factual name) family. Information regarding him and his family was prevalent. I was compelled to be a voice for Matilda.

Now let's go back in time when the country was young and parts still wild. I hope you enjoy the journey.

# CHAPTER 1

Death was coming for her. Her husband, Ira, paced nervously attempting to comfort her. The children stared into the room, confused about what was happening, worried about their mother. She felt their concern. She had been aware of Ira's compassion. If he only knew. If he, for just a moment, could see the memories that had been continuously playing in her mind, he would understand her restlessness. He would know that the pain that kept her in agony had little to do with her physical health, but instead, was a torture within her soul. Memories of death, injustice, and a broken heart that her devoted husband could never heal. God will never spare her. He will never take her from this bed of suffering unless she tells the truth. She must make things right.

"Ira," she could barely whisper, "Ira."

"Yes, Mattie? I'm right here."

"I need to tell you something. Please, sit close to me..."

Less than twenty years earlier, she had been a beautiful sixteen-year-old girl in Clay County, Kentucky with a strong will and a head full of dreams. She was intelligent. Her daddy made sure that she knew how to read. This was rare. In the Appalachian Mountains, women should know their place. Daddy saw things differently. He made sure that she could not only read but could hunt and till the ground as well. "This country is going to war soon, Mattie. We're fighting each other and things could get mighty ugly. I intend to raise a survivor, not just some man's wife."

Her long red hair and green eyes caught the eye of many a

man in those Kentucky hills. But it was her wit and wilderness skills that caught the eye of Billy Akers...the beauty was the icing on the cake.

Billy was the son of Bob Akers. Unlike his father, he was quiet and thoughtful. Forasmuch as he was the apple of his mother's eye, he appeared to be the opposite for his daddy. Bob saw his youngest boy as weak, even though Billy was a better shot and a more successful outdoorsman. Billy's level head and calm demeanor served him well in the woods. Bob was loud, obnoxious, and loved calling attention to himself. He could be found at the general store most afternoons telling one tall tale after another to the local old man's club surrounding the pot-belly stove. Matilda found Bob to be annoying. But Billy? Now he piqued her interest.

Billy had dark hair with matching eyes that always seemed to be thinking. His thick hair lay in loose curls around his collar. He often showed a gentle smile or a soft chuckle, but it was difficult to notice next to his father's large personality. Billy could often be found on the outskirts of a gathering, usually avoiding the unnecessary ribbing from his father.

It was at one of these gatherings at the general store that Billy noticed Matilda Abner. She walked into the store to pick up supplies for her mother who had been ill. Her red hair and green eyes turned many heads, but it was her demeanor that attracted Billy. She walked with confidence, paying no attention to the tall tales being spun around the stove by Bob and his clan. Matilda never looked down when she walked; she always looked straight ahead. And she never asked for help, even with the heavy items.

"Oh, let me help you with that, Miss Abner," Mr. Hobbs offered.

"Thank you, Mr. Hobbs, but I believe I've got it. Could you please add this to Daddy's bill?"

"Yes, ma'am, I'll do that. How's your mama feeling?"

"Mama is feeling a bit better. She wanted me to tell you she'd be in to settle the bill next week."

"Fine, fine, I'm not worried. Tell her I'm glad she's on the mend."

"I will. Thank you again, sir." And with that, she left and began loading her wagon.

Billy approached her as she was gathering her items, "Here, please, let me grab a few things for you. It'll save you some trips."

She turned to protest but then she locked eyes with Billy and thought better of it. A smile sneaked upon her lips, "Thank you. That would be mighty kind of you." Mr. Hobbs smiled, too. He had seen these connections before. He went back to work still grinning to himself.

"I guess I should introduce myself. I'm William Akers, but people call me Billy."

"I know," Matilda said slyly, "you're Bob's boy. But it's very nice to meet you officially Billy. I'm Matilda Abner."

"Yeah, I know," he grinned and looked down. His face began to feel warm, "It's nice to meet you, Miss Abner."

"Please, call me Mattie." They both smiled.

Billy helped her up to her seat on the wagon. "Be careful now. I hope to see you again soon."

"Yes...I hope so, too."

She clucked to her horse, Tucker, who obediently began the trip back to the Abner place. Billy watched the wagon until it disappeared and began planning a way to make sure he would run into her again.

Mattie convinced her mama to let her do her errands for her even after she was well. Every Wednesday she would come into town for supplies, and every Wednesday Billy would make sure he was there. He continued helping her load her wagon, and every week she would talk more and more. Soon he would greet her as she came in and accompany her while she shopped. It was a weekly event they both looked forward to.

One week, Mama came with Mattie to pick out some new fabric. She was also curious as to why Mattie's trips to town were becoming increasingly longer. As Mama stood looking at the new patterns that had come in, Mattie made her way to the grove outside where Billy usually met her. There he sat, grinning at her with his eyes dancing. He loved Wednesdays now. She sat beside him on the grass. They discussed the week's events. Billy had been hunting and killed a buck. He loved how Mattie was not only excited for him but could talk about hunting with him as well as his brothers. She was excited to hear Billy's hunting stories since she had not been able to go lately. She had to help with the garden chores and had been breaking beans all week. She couldn't wait to be done with the harvest so that she could head back into the woods. She loved deer meat, but her favorite was grouse. Bird hunting offered challenges that small game and deer did not and she loved the thrill of getting one for supper. Both she and Billy shared a love of the woods and talked about it often. It wasn't long till they heard the bell of the store door and Mama coming out with her fabric and weekly supplies.

"Mattie, come help me load the wagon now."

"Yes, mama. See you later, Billy."

Billy followed behind her, "Please, let me help you, Mrs. Abner."

"Why thank you, Billy. That's very kind of you."

Billy smiled and helped load the remainder of the items onto the wagon. Mama returned the smile, but as he walked away, a look of concern came across her face. On the way home, Mama approached the subject, "I saw you were talking to Billy Akers. I didn't realize you two know each other."

"We're friends. We like the same things so he's easy to talk to." Mattie didn't elaborate any further, she wasn't quite ready to talk about Billy to anyone else yet.

"Billy is a nice boy, nothing like his father. But you need to be careful, Matilda Grace. The Akers are in a feud with the Caudills and have been for a while now. It's dangerous to be too close to any of them. Do you understand?"

"Yes ma'am," but Mattie said no more. She knew she was too far gone to give up her friendship with Billy. Mama knew that too, but she had to warn her. This wouldn't end well. She could feel it.

The Akers and the Caudills had been feuding for some time. Dr. Caudill, who was rather unstable in mind, had accused one of the Akers of being with his wife. In a jealous rage, he killed the man. The courts declared that he was insane and he left town. Rumor had it that he left the country fleeing to Cuba. The bad blood began to boil. Dr. Caudill returned and they tried him again. This time he was hanged for the crime. The Caudills were infuriated as the law states that you cannot try a man twice for the same crime. But the Akers had too much say in the local politics at the time to allow the mad doctor to live. The bloodshed and destruction from the feud had been going on for years with no end in sight. Mattie was aware of all of this, but the feud couldn't be found in Billy's eyes. He had no interest in being involved. He kept to himself and stayed out of the way. He spoke very little about it. It was as if the Akers were distant kin instead of his own deep-rooted blood.

Despite Mama's warnings, Mattie continued her weekly get-togethers with Billy. There was the first time their hands touched, the first kiss under the big poplar tree, then more serious talks about the future. Their romance had been fairly secret, in their minds anyway. But the locals had been noticing the blossoming love between them. Their folks had noticed, too.

Neither families were thrilled about this development, least of all their fathers. Mr. Abner did not approve of a match that put his daughter into the depths of a nasty feud. Bob Akers had no ill will toward Matilda herself; but her father seemed to think he was better than them. He found his pretentiousness angering and insulting. Regardless of their disapproval, nothing could stop fate. The two wed on the courthouse steps by the justice of the peace without their parents' blessing. As they bonded their union with a kiss, the afternoon sun shone down and the locust cried.

The next few years were happy ones. Mattie and Billy built a house on a plot of land gifted to them by Billy's father. They started a small farm that supplied them with food. Everything that was done was done together, growing vegetables, harvesting, hunting, feeding, and slaughtering their animals. It was a special partnership that grew deeper with each passing year. But as one year grew into two, then four, and now eight, one thing still eluded them...the birth of a child.

This weighed heavily on both of them, but Mattie struggled with it the most. Convinced that there was something wrong with her, she begged God for a child. She imagined their home coming alive with the sound of children. If it was a girl, she would teach her to read and to hunt, to think for herself, just like her daddy taught her. If it was a boy, she hoped he was strong and gentle, like her Billy. Mama told her that she was being punished for her disobedience. Mattie was beginning to believe her. Billy assured her that there was no punishment being handed out for any type of disobedience, regardless of what Mattie's mama said. He was confident that when the time was right, they would be surrounded by their large family of offspring. Until then, they would enjoy each other.

# CHAPTER 2

Frank Prewitt was the local shoe cobbler. He didn't actually live anywhere but could be found everywhere. Billy had seen him in town and asked if he could come by the house and look at some boots that needed mending. Mattie didn't like him. She felt uneasy in his presence. The way he looked at her made her feel uncomfortable. She especially didn't like him inside her home.

"Why hello there, Mrs. Akers. You lookin' pretty as a picture as usual. How you doin'?"

The glint in his eye made Mattie uneasy. The brown streaks of tobacco juice stains on his leathery chin turned her stomach. "Hello, Mr. Prewitt. I'm doing fine, thank you." She hurried away and hoped he would be gone soon.

She much preferred being outside with the animals. She made her rounds to check on them. "Hello there, Sarah!" she called to the white ox in the field. Sarah just stood there and chewed her cud. Mattie secretly named her after her mother-in-law after she criticized the supper that Mattie had prepared for them one night. In front of Billy, she called the ox Bessie so as to not upset him. He did love his mama. The ox didn't seem to mind; she never listened anyway. Deciding to walk a little slower, Mattie bided her time in hopes that the shoes were repaired and the cobbler gone. She daydreamed of holding little hands and showing them the plants and berries; what was safe to eat and what was poison; learning to name the animals of the forest and what they ate and where they hid their babies. Her heart longed for a family of her own.

She made a final stop at the chicken coop to feed the chickens and gather eggs. She walked in the door to find it empty and Frank Prewitt gone. Her body relaxed.

Summer turned to fall and harvest had come and gone. Food had been brought in and meat cured. The hard work of spring and summer had culminated into a comfortable bounty for winter. Christmas was soon approaching.

Mattie awoke to Billy sitting on the edge of the bed. He smiled, "Good morning, sleepyhead. I made you an early Christmas gift. I couldn't wait to give it to you."

Mattie rubbed the sleep out of her eyes and saw Billy was holding a small rattle carved from cedar wood. "Oh, Billy, I love it. It's perfect. I'm so excited, I just can't believe it!"

At Thanksgiving, Mattie had felt poorly. She was so nauseous she could barely eat Mama's delicious cooking. At first, she thought she must be coming down with something, but Mama had asked her, "Could you be with child?"

After eight years, could it be? The doctor had confirmed it and now she relished in her state, upset belly and all.

Billy kissed her forehead, "I'm excited too. I certainly hope the baby gets your looks."

He winked and Mattie smiled, "I love you, Billy Akers."

"I love you, Matilda Akers."

Mattie's heart was full.

"Frank is comin' by to mend some boots for me," Billy called out from the other room as he prepared for his hunting trip. "He'll be here around noon."

Mattie's heart sank. She did not fancy the idea of being alone with Mr. Prewitt. "But you'll be gone...I'll be by myself with him."

Billy laughed good-naturedly, "He's just fixin' my boots,

Mattie, not staying the night. It won't take long and then he'll be gone. I'll be back tomorrow evening. You'll be fine."

Mattie still wasn't happy about it. Billy gave her a kiss and headed out the door. Mattie had seen Frank in town before the holidays. She had caught him watching her. It made her feel uncomfortable; she couldn't wait to get away from him then and certainly couldn't wait until today was over.

Just after noon, there was a rap at the door. Mattie answered it, trying to appear strong, "Good afternoon, Mr. Prewitt, please come in. The boots are right there by the stove."

Frank stepped in looking around, "Much obliged, Mrs. Akers. I'll get right to it then."

Mattie nodded her approval and went back to her sewing. She was taking the seam out of one of her dresses since her waistline was expanding. Frank worked quietly at first, but then began turning his attention toward Mattie,

"Awful lonely out here, ain't it, Mrs. Akers?"

The last thing Mattie wanted was to be friendly with Frank Prewitt, but she had been raised to be polite to others, "Not really. We like the quiet."

Frank smiled and went back to the boots. "Pretty dress you're mendin' there. You wear a lot of pretty dresses. They always look nice with that fiery red hair of yours."

Mattie's hair on the back of her neck stood up and her skin crawled. She could feel his eyes on her. "Thank you, Mr. Prewitt," she said flatly. She left it at that, best not to encourage him with more conversation and she had hoped her tone would hint that she was not in the mood for his chitter-chatter. She continued sewing, hoping to conceal her discomfort. Good lord! When will he ever get done with those silly boots!

"Billy out hunting? Awful quiet around here."

She really did not want to admit he wasn't close by, but it wasn't very Christian to lie. "Yes sir, he is. He's deer hunting up at Tar Ridge." She immediately regretted releasing that information. Her nerves had gotten the better of her.

"Ohhh, up at Tar Ridge! That's a good piece away. Good

hunting up there though. I may have to come back and finish these boots. I didn't bring enough supplies. If he's in Tar Ridge he won't be back till at least tomorrow. I reckon he won't be needing them by mornin'."

Mattie was already dreading tomorrow knowing that Frank would have to return. "That'll be fine Mr. Prewitt. Tomorrow morning will be fine."

Frank smiled at her with his tobacco-stained teeth, "Thank you, ma'am. I do apologize. It was a bigger job than I expected. I'll see you tomorrow, about the same time then." He made his way to the door and let himself out.

"Thank you, Mr. Prewitt. We'll see you tomorrow."

"You'll see me tomorrow." He turned around and tipped his hat then walked down the road towards town. Mattie shivered and closed the door. The room felt lighter.

The remainder of the day was uneventful. Mattie finished altering one dress and started on another. She was looking forward to her belly beginning to grow. She was just barely showing. She wanted to feel the baby moving inside of her; she couldn't wait for tiny kicks to wake her up in the night. She did lie down for just a bit when her stomach began feeling exceptionally queasy. She fed the animals, said hello to Bessie, and sat down for supper with some warmed-up biscuits and honey. That sounded like something that her stomach could handle and since she was only feeding herself this evening, she indulged. The house was quiet when Billy was away hunting. But Mattie decided to enjoy the quiet this evening. Soon their lives would be completely different, and quiet nights will be nonexistent. After supper, she sat by the oil lamp continuing alterations on her dresses. She imagined her little boy in her arms, all swaddled in blue. Billy would tell him hunting stories and Mattie would sing him to sleep. She imagined her little girl, dressed in her pretty dress for church. Billy would call her his little sunshine. It would all be so beautiful. She wished Billy was here to share her daydreams with. She felt a tinge of loneliness, but she was not alone…

# CHAPTER 3

Frank Prewitt had walked down the road that afternoon until he was out of sight of the Akers place. He made a left turn into the woods. It was winter, the foliage was gone except for the pines. He was sure he could find a patch close to their house to wait out the daylight. The cold December air was biting, but Frank was on fire. Every nerve in his body felt alive.

He watched the day slowly dim. He could see Mattie sitting in her chair mending her dresses. As Mattie doused the oil lamp and climbed into bed, Frank was inching closer to the lonely cabin. The night was dark, only a sliver of moon lit up the sky. He felt confident enough to wait just outside her window until she was asleep. He sat in the grass with the excitement of a child at Christmas. Just a little while longer and he will get what he came for...Matilda Akers.

Mattie awoke with a start. She wasn't sure if she was dreaming or if she had heard a noise in the front room. Lying very still she listened, another creak. There was movement in the front of the house.

"Billy? Is that you?"

Frank froze. She was awake. He stood perfectly still and waited.

Mattie got up. Billy must have come home, maybe he was ill or hurt. She went to check on him. She walked into the sitting room and saw no one, "Billy?"

Suddenly her mouth was covered as she was grabbed from behind. She fought to get away, every muscle in her body tense and flailing.

"Shh, shh, shhhh...be still. Don't make me hurt you. Hold

still."

The smell of tobacco, sweat, and body odor was pressed up against her. She had no idea who was in her home right now but, by god, she was not going down easy. His hand slipped on her face enough that she could bite him and she did, hard. She tasted his blood as he screamed out and jerked his hand away.

"Dammit, you bitch!" He grabbed her by the hair and threw her to the ground.

She tried kicking him, but with her bare feet, the blows didn't faze him. He kicked her hard in the thigh. His boots made hard contact again as he began kicking her groin and stomach. She screamed and tried to protect herself; one of the kicks made contact with her face. She was still conscious but everything felt hazy. The world went numb. Reality seemed irrelevant. She was unsure of what was happening.

"That took the fight out of you."

She felt her nightgown being pulled up and her panties removed. This couldn't be happening. This couldn't be real. Then she felt the hard thrust between her thighs. On the wooden plank floor, every thrust rammed her body into the hard boards. She felt as though her insides were ripping. The gravity of her situation was beginning to sink in, the blow to her face fading. He continued having his way with her,

"That's a good girl..."

Mattie was regaining her senses. That voice. She knew that voice. The fight in her returned. She realized her arms were free, taking both hands she reached up to his face and clawed hard!

"DAMMIT!"

He backhanded her but the adrenaline was pumping through Mattie's veins, the hit didn't faze her. She began violently struggling to get away.

"You shouldn't have done that, Miss Mattie."

She could hear the sneer. But she now knew who she was dealing with. It was Frank Prewitt. The rage in her boiled. He turned her over onto her belly and penetrated her again. The pain caused Mattie to scream.

"That's right, little girl."

She could hear him getting close to climax. His breath quickened and he called out. She wanted to vomit but she could feel his grip loosen. She remembered the ax leaning against the wall, it was within arm's reach. Thinking he had beaten the fight out of her, he let go. He was wrong. He pulled away from her. Mattie grabbed the ax and with all the strength she could muster from the depth of her soul, for herself and for her child, she swung hard, landing the blow squarely on the side of Frank's head. He crumpled to the ground. He was moaning and the ax bounced back. She hadn't been able to see what end she hit him with. As she felt for the blade Mattie realized she had hit him with the blunt end of the ax. He would regain himself soon. She turned the ax around and swung down with all of her strength. She felt contact, the spray of blood. She jerked the ax up hard and swung again. A crunching sound, blood spray, the ax stuck to the floor. Mattie staggered back. A metallic taste filled her mouth, the smell of copper in the air, she stumbled outside and fell to her knees. The vomit came violently. She collapsed on her side, feeling the pain of the brutal attack throughout her body, her intimate places defiled. She curled up on the porch and wept.

Empty of tears, Mattie sat on the floor of the front porch surrounded by the quiet of the night. She kept her back against the outside wall of the house. She wanted no more surprises. She was numb, frozen. Staring at the darkness, she tried to digest what had just happened. She could feel the sticky moistness of the blood. She couldn't make herself go back inside for fear that Frank Prewitt was awaiting her return. A sense of emptiness overwhelmed her. There was no doubt that her long-awaited baby was dead. She knew it. The baby she had longed to hold for so long will now fly with the angels. The man who she knew to lay dead in her house, would rot in Hell.

The sun rose. It was inevitable. Time doesn't stop for tragedy or sin. Mattie watched the light slowly fill the sky, emotionless.

"Lord, I think I've killed a man. I'm not sorry. I don't want your forgiveness. I just want to know why...why did you let this happen?" She laid her hand on her belly, "I'm so sorry, little one."

She struggled to her feet and turned to face what was inside. She stared down at Frank's head completely separated from his body. Her aim had been true. He would not be coming after her again. The sight of him was morbid and messy, the bloodstains covering most of the floor; splatter was on the walls and ceilings. Anyone else would be ill from the sight of it all, but Mattie felt nothing. She staggered to the washbasin, pain coursing through her body. The small mirror told the tale of her harrowing night. Her eyes were turning blue, her nose was swollen almost black, dried blood covered her jaw and cheeks. Looking down at her nightgown covered with patches of dried blood, she noticed the puddle forming at her feet. It was dripping from between her legs.

Mattie's legs gave out. The cramping in her abdomen was intense. "Please, God...no," but her whispered prayer was ignored. With one last great pain she cried out and a large clot of blood and tissue passed onto the floor. The pain stopped. The baby was gone.

# CHAPTER 4

Billy started home earlier than he had expected. He had snagged a deer and some small game. With plenty of time to clean and prepare them, he decided that should be plenty of meat for a while. He hadn't liked leaving Mattie alone in her condition. Besides, he had some projects to work on at home.

As he got closer to the little cabin, an uneasiness fell over him. Something bad was in the air, evil forebodings are what the Bible called them. Probably just worry over his pregnant wife, but, he found it difficult to shake the feeling.

It seemed eerily quiet at the old home place. There was no sign of activity anywhere.

"Mattie?"

Dried blood covered the front porch with a large coagulation of blood collected by the door.

"Oh my god," Billy whispered to himself. "Mattie!"

He threw open the front door. The smell of copper hung heavy in the air. There was more blood. Stepping in the doorway, he stood in disbelief as he saw Frank Prewitt's head and lifeless body in the front room. Prewitt's eyes were open and staring upward, large gashes on his face.

"MATTIE!!"

He ran into the other room and found Mattie slumped on the floor; a fresh puddle of blood soaking the midsection of her gown. Her face was barely recognizable.

"No. No...no...no..." he cradled his wife in his arms. She was still breathing.

"Dear God...what has happened?"

Billy had to blot out the gruesome scene for the time being

and tend to his wife and her injuries. He removed her blood-stained nightgown and cleaned her off, trying to ascertain her injuries. Her nose was broken and her eyes black. There was severe bruising all along her torso and chest. She had been bleeding from both her vagina and buttocks.

"What did he do to you?"

Billy laid Mattie in the bed with a fresh nightgown. He couldn't leave her to go get the doctor and certainly couldn't bring the doctor here with the scene in the front room. He placed a blanket over her and kissed her forehead. He had to deal with the carnage now. Looking down at Prewitt's empty eyes, the ax still stuck to the floorboards, he seethed. The injuries to his wife, the blood running down her thighs, he had done that. Mattie had said she was uncomfortable with him there and Billy had ignored her.

"This is my fault."

Rage burned. He reared back and kicked the body of Frank Prewitt with all his might. "That's for my wife and baby, you son of a bitch!"

Billy had no idea when Mattie might regain consciousness or even if she would. What he did know was that he had to dispose of Frank and fast. He dumped the remainder of the potatoes out of their burlap sack and used it to store the head. He brought Bessie to the front of the house. Using an old quilt, he wrapped up Frank's body and then secured it with rope. Billy tossed the body across the back of Bessie. He tied up the burlap sack and secured it to the body along with a shovel. Patting Bessie on the neck he took the lead rope, "C'mon, girl. We need to get back before Mattie wakes up." He began walking toward the wood line with Bessie slowly meandering behind him, completely unaware of the evil load she carried.

The cold December temperatures and quiet woods helped to clear Billy's mind. Mattie's brutalized body, the blood, the dead man he was getting ready to hide, it was all so surreal. Time was of the essence. This had to be done quickly so that he could get back to his wife; she needed him. She needed him to help her heal; she needed him to protect her. He knew he had no choice but to hide Frank's body and the crime against his wife. There was a feud and Frank was a distant relative of the Caudills. Billy had done well to avoid involvement in the fighting, but this would ignite the fire they needed to start trouble with his family. Mattie could be in danger. Then the idea of people looking at Mattie differently, with pity or worse, with blame. He would have none of it. The sooner he could put this behind them and move forward, the better.

He walked deep into the woods until he found a clearing within a grove of trees. This is the spot. He grabbed the shovel secured to Frank's body and began digging. The ground was frozen and proved to be a challenge to dig. Six feet would be impossible right now with just him and a shovel. He will have to come back during the thaw and bury him deeper. That was not the scenario that Billy had hoped for.

After preparing a space a little over three feet deep, Billy tossed Frank's body into it. He placed his head at his feet as a sign of disrespect.

"Rot in Hell, bastard."

There would be no last rights for Frank Prewitt. Billy surveyed the covered grave. It was certainly not as deep as he would like. He attempted to cover it with brush. With any luck, a bear or a pack of coyotes might decide to dig him up for supper. Would serve the son of a bitch right.

Bessie stood waiting, oblivious to the events happening around her. Equally oblivious was she of the trail of blood going down her side. A stark contrast against the white oxen's hide. Billy took the lead rope and began the trek home. He had to get back to Mattie.

Mattie hadn't moved and was still lying in the bed, just as Billy had left her, her breathing slow and light. There was an air of relief, Billy did not want her to awaken to the gruesome mess from the night's harrowing events. Billy worked hard to clean it up, taking him hours. All the while, Mattie lay sleeping. There was no getting the traces of blood out of the wood floor.

He would have to replace the planks, but at least the bulk of the mess was gone and the furniture back in place. He had cleaned the ax and placed it back where he always kept it. Maybe it would be best to keep things as normal as possible. He pulled up a chair close to where Mattie lay and waited.

As the moon hung high above, Mattie began to stir. Billy had nodded off in his chair and her low moans had startled him awake.

"Mattie? Are you awake?"

She barely moved her head, her legs inched slightly. Billy waited anxiously, but then the moaning stopped and her slow rhythmic breathing returned.

"That's something I reckon." It had to be a good sign.

Just before dawn, Mattie began moaning and speaking. Billy couldn't understand what she was saying. He had made himself a bed on the floor next to her so that he could hear her if she awoke. He sat on the chair. The moonlight was streaming through the window reflecting off of her beaten face. Billy could see that her eyes were still swollen shut. He placed his hand on her arm,

"Mattie it's me. Wake up, honey."

Billy gently shook her arm, "Mattie, wake up."

Mattie's eyes could barely open. She let out a blood-curdling scream. "No! No! No! Get away from me! No! Stop!"

Her body tense, she flattened herself against the wall in terror. The reaction startled Billy and his heart broke for her.

"Mattie, honey, it's me. It's Billy. You're safe, Mattie. I'm here. You're safe."

Mattie looked around in complete confusion, "Where's Frank?! Frank has to leave! Get him out of here, Billy! Please!!"

Billy continued to console his wife, "He's gone, Mattie. Frank is gone. He will never hurt you again. He's gone."

Mattie's face looked wild. But as she began to realize that she was no longer in danger, she began to cry. Deep, penetrating sobs escaped her broken body. The cries continued for a long time. All the while, Billy slowly stroked her hair.

When Mattie stopped crying, she didn't speak. She lay on her side facing the wall. She wouldn't look at her husband or talk to him. She just stared blankly. She was numb. Billy stayed by her side but let her be. He didn't know what he could say to console her. What she seemed to need now was her space and some rest.

Billy sat by her side till the sun shone through their windows. At times her breathing was slow and steady and he hoped that she may have been sleeping. Maybe a little breakfast would help; Mattie needed to regain her strength. As Billy began frying some bacon and scrambling some eggs, he was haunted by the terror in Mattie's eyes, the way she had shut down. He may never know exactly what happened or what she went through, the horror of it all. The thought of Frank Prewitt lying in the cold ground with no proper burial, his head at his feet gave him some peace. He brought a small plate of scrambled eggs to Mattie in hopes that she might eat a little something.

"Mattie," he spoke softly, "I made you some eggs."

Her eyes were open but there was no response.

"You should try to eat. If not for you, for the baby."

"The baby is gone," she said flatly.

Billy was dumbstruck. His whole world was crashing down.

"Are you sure? Maybe you're wrong, Mattie..."

"I'm not," she snapped abruptly.

Billy was frozen. His wife brutalized. Their baby gone. There were no words.

"I'm going to set these eggs here on the night table. I'll step out and let you rest. I'm so sorry Mattie. I'm so sorry," and with that, he walked outside in the direction of his woodshop.

The woodshop was a small shack where Billy did his woodworking. It was where he liked to go to think. Mattie never came inside unless Billy gave her the ok, just in case he was making a gift for her. He enjoyed surprising her. Today his little sanctuary felt like a tomb. He looked at the small cradle that sat lonely on the floor, anxiously awaiting a baby to hold. On his work table, a Noah's Ark with several carved animals sat ready to be painted. It was all too much. The fury began to swell from deep within. Wood began flying toward the wall; he punched his fists repeatedly on the table, blood running down his arm. Collapsing to the floor by the cradle, he called out to the God that seemed nowhere to be found.

"Why?! Why?! Why did you let this happen?? Where were you dammit!!"

Billy cupped his face in his hands and wept.

The next few weeks, Mattie improved slowly. She said very little but had begun to eat and her face was beginning to heal. They slept in separate beds as Mattie couldn't stand the idea of being touched. She wrote a letter to her mama explaining that she had lost the baby and that she was too ill to come for Christmas, assuring her she would be over as soon as she felt up to it. Billy visited his parents for Christmas without her, giving them the same explanation as to Mattie's absence. Everyone seemed to understand. Then one day, Billy walked into the cabin to find Mattie cooking him supper. She looked up at him trying to smile while tears began slowly falling down her cheeks. Billy's heart broke anew for her. He slowly walked over to her and gently placed his hand on her back. She turned toward him, burying her head in his chest, releasing her grief from her recent tragedies. That night he held her while she slept.

# CHAPTER 5

Curtis Shearer's old coonhound, Jack, was roaming the woods like he often did. He had chased a rabbit for quite a ways until the little fella ducked into a burrow. Jack continued his exploring in hopes of finding something else that interested him. There was a scent that was getting his attention. With his nose to the ground, he was getting closer to the source. Whatever it was, he was sure it was under some loose dirt in a grove of trees. He started digging. Dirt and pieces of burlap flew underneath him. Old Jack found his treasure. Proudly he trotted back home with his new find. Mrs. Shearer was in for a surprise.

❅ ❅ ❅

"Where is he?" Mattie needed to know what happened to Frank. Her memory was a blur.

"He's gone." is all Billy knew to say to her.

"Will he be back?"

Billy was surprised that she didn't know or remember what happened that night. "No. He won't be back...ever."

He took his wife's hands in his, "What do you remember, Mattie?"

She looked down, unable to look him in the eye, "He hurt me, Billy. He hurt me bad. He killed our baby. I'm not sure when it stopped; he must have knocked me unconscious."

Billy wrapped his arms around his wife, thankful that he had been able to clean everything up before she could see the morbid scene. Whatever happened that night, at least part of it is unknown to her. He only wished all of it was and that the baby they long-awaited was still growing in her belly.

* * *

Curtis Shearer was on his way back to his place with the sheriff, "Doris took one look at it and went straight to the ground I tell ya! Took me pouring a bucket of water over her head to bring her back."

Sheriff Lawson found Curtis' story to be far-fetched but found it hard to believe that he could make up such a tale, "You really think its Frank Prewitt's HEAD??"

"Not a doubt in my mind. Ol' Jack was licking on it like a meat bone. I nearly lost my breakfast!"

This would be the first incident of its kind in the history of Clay County. Sheriff Lawson wasn't sure what to expect.

They arrived at the Shearer home. Doris was looking pale on the porch.

"I moved it into the tool shed out of sight of Doris. She's mighty upset."

He opened the door and just inside was the partially decomposed head of Frank Prewitt the shoe cobbler. Even with the decomposition and damage done by Jack, there was no denying his identity.

"Where on Earth did your dog find this?"

"I'm not rightly sure," a look of concern on Curtis' face, "but the closest farm is the Akers'."

Curtis gave the sheriff a burlap sack to place the head in. They tied it to the sheriff's saddle and Lawson mounted his horse. "I'm gonna take a ride, Curtis, and see what I can find. I'll be checking back with you. Tell Doris I'm awfully sorry she had to witness that," he clucked to his horse and headed toward the woods and the Akers homestead.

Naturally following the path of least resistance, Bullet carried the sheriff through the woods that separated the Shearer and Akers place. Lawson thought it best to let Bullet take the lead as that would seem what anyone trying to hide a body in a hurry might choose. The wooded area that he was searching was expansive and he held little hope of finding the rest of the body. As the pair slowly traversed the terrain and searched for anything that looked unnatural, Lawson spotted a grove of trees. Leading Bullet in that direction he could see that within them was a small flat plot of land.

"Hmm, interesting," he muttered to himself.

He secured Bullet to a tree and made his way to the center of the grove to check it out. He spotted a freshly dug hole that may have been made by a dog. The earth had been recently disturbed around it. Strange, considering the ground was usually frozen this time of year. Squatting down he began to widen the hole that appeared to have been started by Jack. He uncovered a small piece of blanket, then the toe of a boot. His mouth dropped, "Jesus, you gotta be kidding me."

Rushing back to his horse to retrieve his spade, Lawson could feel his adrenaline pumping. Carefully, he cleared away the soil revealing something long, wrapped in an old quilt. It was the length of a man's body.

It was almost dark by the time the sheriff got back to town. He was actually glad it was so late. The town was quiet at sundown and he didn't want the questions and rumors circulating. Lawson's first stop was the mortuary. Marcus Gabbard had been the undertaker for years and lived above. He stared at Lawson in disbelief as the story of the day's events was replayed.

"Oddest thing," the sheriff shared with Gabbard, "his head had been buried at his feet. Whoever did this, there was hate behind it."

He unloaded the body and head and got them inside the mortuary for preparation, "Save the quilt, his clothing, and any other material that you find. I found some shreds of a sack so be on the lookout for more of that as well."

He left Marcus with Frank's remains; he needed to go to the jail to feed the only prisoner he had, an old drunk named Gene who would be released tomorrow for disorderly conduct.

Not much happened around Clay County, Gene had been the only resident of the jail for the last month or so. This was uncharted territory.

It was the wee hours of the morning before Sheriff Lawson was able to fall asleep. Who in the world would want to kill Frank Prewitt? Admittedly, he wasn't the most likable fellow, but he had never gotten in trouble before or had any altercations that he was aware of. Plus, to bury him with his head at his feet? Whoever killed him had zero respect for the man. Trying to figure out why he had been buried on the Akers place was unsettling. It was hard to imagine Billy ever doing anything like that. He was a good ol' boy, quiet and polite, nothing like his father. He would have to go to their house tomorrow and let them know what he discovered. Lawson figured that Mattie would be terrified knowing that someone had hidden such a gruesome thing on their property.

The morning sun was shining. Billy could see Sheriff Lawson riding up the road and his heart sank. Panic began to consume him; he had to pull it together.

"Calm down. It's going to be ok." He had to concentrate on protecting Mattie, that's all that mattered. He walked down the road and threw up his hand to the approaching lawman.

"Good mornin'! How are you doin' today?" He welcomed him warmly although inside he was terrified.

"Well Billy, I've been better. I got some bad news for you."

Billy was worried that this could have something to do with the feud.

"Is Daddy alright?"

"Oh yeah, as far as I know. Nothing about your family. It appears that someone has murdered Frank Prewitt and buried his body on your property. His head was cut clean off. They even buried his head at his feet. Whoever did it was certainly trying to settle a score. Wanted to let you know and ask you when was the last time you might have seen Frank and if there's been anyone hanging around that you've noticed. Maybe someone who asked permission to hunt on your land or something?"

Billy was hoping the fear he felt inside was coming off as shock, "Are you serious? My God that's awful! Yeah, it's been a while since I've seen Frank, back in the fall I reckon."

Sheriff Lawson pondered for a moment, "Mind if I look around your place, just see if I see anything that might help me to figure out what happened?"

Billy wished the good Lord would take him right there, "Absolutely, be my guest. Mattie is at her ma and pa's visiting and I'm just working in my woodshed. If you need anything just let me know."

Lawson nodded and thanked him; he tied up his horse and began walking around the property to see if there were any clues as to how Frank ended up in the predicament he found himself in.

Billy went to the woodshed where he would be out of sight and could pull himself together. He hadn't lied to the sheriff-he didn't kill Frank. But he did bury him and it's likely that Mattie was the one who dealt the deadly blow. She has no memory of what happened, no recollection of how Frank Prewitt disappeared. She may even think that Billy did it. The things that man did to her, the death of their baby; he deserved to be buried like that and he deserved to die as he did. But people cannot know what happened to Mattie or that she killed him. They can't know anything. Billy knew he had to keep it together. Soon this will be over and they can go on with their lives. He smoothed over his face with his hands and tried to remember to breathe.

# CHAPTER 6

Sheriff Lawson walked the property, nothing looked out of place. He was admiring the large white ox Bessie when he noticed some odd markings. He approached her. There seemed to be a brownish stain that ran from just behind her shoulder to the bottom of her belly. Bessie just stood there chewing her cud. "It's been dry for a while, I don't know why she'd have mud on her side like that. It would be on her legs." He wet his finger with his spit to see if it came off. The stain began to flake.

"That's odd."

Lawson knew mud would not flake off like that. But something else would…blood. He saw that Billy was still in the woodshed so he decided to search inside the house. In order to avoid tipping him off to his suspicions, Lawson slipped in the back door. Everything looked in order. He walked through the house looking around carefully. In the front room, he saw the ax leaning up against the wall. Everyone kept an ax handy, but there were new boards replaced on the floor not far from where the ax was stored. Could this be where Frank had met his demise? Nothing else looked incriminating. There was a sack of potatoes on the floor. Lawson noticed the picture and name, the same brand he and his wife bought.

"Guess I better ask Billy a couple of questions," he said to himself as he set his sights on the woodshed.

"Hey, Billy! You got a minute?"

Billy stepped out appearing to be at ease. He was thankful no one could see what was happening on the inside.

"Hey, Billy, have you noticed a stain on Bessie there? It flakes up like blood."

Billy felt the color in his face slowly drain. He needed to come up with an explanation quickly because, no, he had not seen that. How did he miss that??

"Oh yeah, I slaughtered a pig and gave it to the Shearers as a thank you for helping me put a new roof on the barn. I hadn't paid any attention that Bessie still had a stain on her."

He hoped he sounded believable. He had slaughtered a pig for the Shearers but it had been over the summer.

"Oh, I see," the sheriff nodded in understanding. "Thanks, Billy, I'll head out. I appreciate your cooperation."

"Sure thing, sheriff. Happy to help."

Lawson unhitched his horse and headed to the undertaker to see if the items found on Frank Prewitt were ready for his inspection. He had a lot of thinking to do.

"Hey, Marcus, got anything for me?" The sheriff was hoping the articles found on the body would clear things up.

"I have everything for you there on the floor. There's a lot of dried blood and there were some scraps from what looks to be a potato sack, but that's about it."

Lawson went to the stack and saw the scraps on top of some old clothes and a quilt, "Thanks, Marcus. I'll take these with me. Have you spoken with any of the Caudills? They are related to Frank, cousins I think. They can help with the next of kin. I can ride up there if you like."

Marcus agreed that it would be best if Lawson went and spoke with the Caudill family. The feud had everyone a little on edge when it came to dealing with some of the Caudills and Akers. Marcus Gabbard didn't want to be caught in any crossfire.

"Sure Marcus, I'll head up after I get a bite to eat. I want to look through these belongings as well. I appreciate your help."

"You're welcome, sheriff, anytime."

Marcus was right, everything was covered in blood. Lawson looked over the quilt carefully. The binding and material gave no hint as to where it might have come from. The clothing told an interesting story. There were rips in the shirt which might mean there was some form of struggle before he died.

Lawson hoped there might be more indication of that when Marcus was done with the body. As he spread the pieces of burlap out, a design caught his eye. It was the image of a raccoon tail and a bit of green just below it. The same as found on the Gun Man potato sack label. Gun Man Potatoes used a pioneer man wearing a coonskin cap and a green shirt as its logo. This matched what Sheriff Lawson was seeing on this piece. He knew it well, it was the same brand of potatoes that his wife used. It was also the same potatoes that Mattie and Billy had in their kitchen.

Sheriff Lawson was turning the evidence over in his head as he rode out to the Caudill farm. He wasn't sure what this news might set off. He had to choose his words carefully to avoid retaliation. Although some of the evidence was pointing toward Billy as a possible suspect, Lawson had to admit that his complicity in allowing him to look around his place worked in his favor. It was hard for him to believe that Billy would hurt anyone. He had done well avoiding the feud altogether and had never been in trouble.

As he found himself within earshot of the Caudill cabin, he began to shout out, "Hey Dan! Dan Caudill! You home, Dan?" It was wise to announce your presence early in case there was any paranoia in the air.

"Who's askin'?"

"It's Sheriff Lawson, I need to talk to you."

Lawson placed himself and his horse in the open so that he was easily seen.

"Oh hey, sheriff. C'mon up and have a seat." Bad feuds do not necessarily equate to bad people.

"How ya doin', Dan? Sorry to bother you but I've got some disturbing news. We found Frank Prewitt's body yesterday. It was buried in a shallow grave. He'd been murdered. I'm investigating but I still have no idea what happened. I was thinking you were some relation to him and didn't know if you could help with contacting his closest of kin?" He was hoping to avoid giving too much information because getting a Caudill stirred up was asking for trouble.

"You don't say? I can't say that I'm surprised. Frank was an asshole. We may have been kin, but I didn't care for him. He's got a sister in Tennessee, I can get in touch with her for you. Where'd you find him?"

Sheriff Lawson approached the subject cautiously, "Well, he was buried on Billy Akers's farm. I'm still trying to figure out how he got there."

Dan looked at Lawson curiously, "Billy's place, eh? That's interesting don't you think?"

"Well now Dan, we don't want to jump to any conclusions. Anybody could have taken him up there. I'm still investigating. Plus Billy was awfully cooperative, gave me free rein to look around." Lawson hoped that would pacify him for now. "Did Frank have any enemies that you know of?"

"Hmph," Dan snorted, "plenty of 'em. He had a tendency to piss people off. I don't know of anyone who would want to kill him though."

Lawson got up and stepped off the porch, "If I come up with anything I'll let you know. Thanks for volunteering to contact Frank's sister for me. I'll be in touch." Sheriff Lawson got up on his horse and headed back to town. He wanted to check back in with Marcus Gabbard before he called it a day.

Marcus was in the back cleaning up when Joe walked in, "Be right out!" he yelled from the back, "Hey there Joe, I was just finishing up. There was some strange stuff on Frank for sure. Definitely some sort of fight or scuffle before he died. Come back here and I'll show you." They walked to the room where the body had been prepared, "Look here on his hand, a whole chunk of it is missing. Almost like a bite. Now see here on his cheeks, there are some deep claw marks, on both sides. Kind of looks like someone may have been fighting him off. It doesn't appear to be from an animal. Hard to say though."

Joe looked at the marks on Frank's face and the injury on his hand. He had to agree with Marcus.

"How do you think he was decapitated?"

"Well, it appears," Marcus took another look at the head and the top of the shoulders to verify, "It was probably with an ax. The way the bones were broken appears to have been sudden. He was alive when it happened; there are no other injuries that would cause his death. The unevenness makes me think it took more than one swing."

Sheriff Lawson was more perplexed than ever. Billy had looked like a suspect, however, he would have been able to overpower Frank with little to no effort. Whoever was fighting off Frank was either smaller than him or completely taken off guard, yet they were strong enough to completely decapitate him with an ax. Lawson had no more clue of who killed Frank now than he did when he first discovered the head at the Shearers' place.

Dan Caudill had been contemplating the discovery of Frank's body on Billy Akers's farm all afternoon. He had gone for a walk in the woods to clear his head and found he was making his way to his cousin Charles' farm. This situation might just open up an opportunity, as the Bible says: an eye for an eye. Charles Caudill and his family had just finished supper when he arrived. Charles' wife, Esther, insisted on fixing Dan a plate. Esther was quite a cook so Dan didn't mind the invite at all. After filling his belly with fried grouse, soup beans, collard greens, and cornbread, he thanked Esther and excused himself and Charles to take a little walk.

"Charles, an opportunity has presented itself that might be too good to pass up. The sheriff stopped by to let me know that they found Frank's body yesterday. He's been murdered."

Charles stopped walking, "No shit?! Murdered? I mean, Frank had a way about him. It wouldn't surprise me if someone wanted to whip his ass, but murder? I wouldn't have expected that."

Dan nodded in agreement and continued, "Yeah, I feel the same, but here's the thing. They found his body on Billy Akers's farm. Seems awfully suspicious to me."

Charles pondered on this a moment, "It does, don't it? I

find it hard to see Billy killing anybody though. He's soft."

Dan looked hard at his cousin, "He's still an Akers, Charlie. Even if he wasn't the one who killed Frank, I guarantee he knew about it. Somebody's gotta pay. Somebody's gotta pay for Eli's death."

Charles looked down; he knew Dan was right. Elijah Caudill had been shot down in cold blood on his farm just a few weeks ago, leaving his wife and kids alone. It was unknown who had killed him but they knew it was an Akers and had been contemplating retaliation. This feud never stopped destroying families.

"You're right," Charles admitted. He knew something had to be done.

"Besides," Dan continued, "going after Billy will be going after Bob. I hate that son of a bitch."

Boston Bob was a huge player on the Akers side. Somebody had to take him down. Dan and Charles began hatching their plan for revenge.

# CHAPTER 7

Mattie was gathering her things together in anticipation of Billy's arrival. She had stayed with her folks for the past month. Billy thought it would be good for her to spend some time with her mama and heal from the loss of the baby and the injuries inflicted on her at the hands of Frank Prewitt. Mattie had lied about her facial injuries saying that the blood loss from the miscarriage had made her light-headed and that she fell, hitting the corner of the cast iron stove.

"Matilda Grace!! You are lucky to be alive! I can't believe you didn't go to a doctor. Billy should have insisted. You are so stubborn, just like your daddy."

Her mother had scolded her, but Mattie was relieved that she believed the lie. It was nice to rest and eat Mama's cooking but she was homesick and had been missing Billy terribly.

Billy arrived in the late morning. Mattie felt like something was off but couldn't quite put her finger on it. He still greeted her with the same smile that won her over years earlier, but there was something in his eyes, worry perhaps.

"Everything ok back home?" She was hoping that maybe he would give her some insight.

"Things are good," he lied, "will be better now that you'll be back."

His sly grin melted her heart, just like the first day they met.

After loading her things and some goodies that Mr. and Mrs. Abner put together for them, canned vegetables from the fall harvest, and cured deer meat, they said their goodbyes and headed home. Billy had to tell Matilda what had happened while she was gone; about finding Frank Prewitt's decapitated body on their farm and the sheriff coming by to ask questions. He just wasn't sure how to bring it up, nor was he sure how she would take it. She had still been unable to remember what happened to Frank that night.

The ride home was quiet. Billy enjoyed the warmth of Mattie next to him. The fears and worries seemed far away as he listened to her tell stories of her father's hunting trips and her mother's scolding. When she laughed, it calmed the sense of foreboding that had been haunting him. He knew that when he sat her down to catch her up on what had been going on, her light, easy mood would change. He feared that he would lose her again, that she would shut down like before. That was unbearable to watch. Billy had felt so helpless.

After settling in, Billy sat Mattie down, "We need to talk, Mattie. Some things happened while you were gone and I need to prepare you for them."

Mattie's heart sank. She had fooled herself into feeling normal again, but the last few months had been anything but.

"The sheriff came by last week. He found Frank Prewitt's body. Mattie, I found Frank dead. I buried his body in the woods. The sheriff was asking a lot of questions. He will probably come by again any day and want to ask you some questions as well."

Mattie sat emotionless. Her eyes focused on the ax in the corner. Flashes of memories came to her in still-frame scenes. The smell of tobacco and body odor. His hand across her mouth, the fear, the fight, the rape, and then...the survival. She remembered what he did to her, raping her. How she seized the opportunity and with all of her might, swung the ax. The feel of connection. The ax stuck in the floor. The smell. It was all there.

"Mattie," Billy whispered softly, "are you ok?"

She turned slowly to face him, "I killed him. I killed Frank Prewitt." The tears came like a raging river. Her sobs shook her to her very soul. All Billy could do was hold her and let her get it out. He had known Mattie had killed Frank but hearing her say it confirmed the graveness of their situation.

When Mattie had released all of her tears, she leaned motionless into Billy's arms. She was unable to speak. When the words came, they were slow and heavy.

"I fought so hard. After he came to work on your shoes, he left and said he would be back the next day, that he needed more supplies. In the middle of the night, I heard someone come in. I thought it was you. I got up to see and he grabbed me from behind. He threw me on the floor. Oh, Billy...he did terrible things to me. I fought him. I bit him, I clawed him, I kicked, I screamed. He kicked me...my face, my stomach. He had his way with me. He raped me like a dog, Billy. I couldn't make him stop. I saw the ax and it was within reach. I grabbed it and swung, hard. I hit him on the side of the head with the blunt end. It stunned him, but I had to kill him. He would have killed me, I just know it. I took the blade and swung down as hard as I could, twice. I couldn't even see where I was swinging; I just knew he went silent. Oh, Billy..." She wept softly now.

Billy held her, tears streaming down his face. This was his fault. He knew she didn't like being alone with Frank. He ignored her and had him come over anyway. If he had listened to his wife, paid attention to her fears, she would not have gone through this. The baby would still be on its way. Frank would still be alive, unfortunately, but he wouldn't have had the opportunity to hurt Mattie. There was a feeling of impending doom.

"I am so sorry, Mattie," Billy was still fighting back tears. "This is all my fault. I am so sorry."

Mattie looked at her husband placing her hand on his cheek, "No, Billy, it's Frank's fault. He did this. He did all of it."

They held each other as dusk turned to night.

In the early morning hours, Billy and Mattie remained in the same spot in the front room. Neither had said a word, both looking at the ax leaned up against the wall in the corner. Billy broke the silence.

"We have to make a plan, Mattie. Sheriff Lawson will be back and we have to know what we are going to say."

"I'm gonna tell him the truth. I'm gonna tell him what

Frank did and that I defended myself."

Billy sat up, "No. No. Absolutely not. Do you have any idea what will happen to you if you do that?? Frank was a Caudill, Mattie. This will put you in the feud, a bounty on your head. Any idea what the court hearing will be like?? Everything he did to you sitting there in judgment by the rest of the town! Spending your whole life being the woman who killed Frank Prewitt? That is if the Caudills let you live. No, no I won't allow it!" Billy was adamant.

"What else can we do, Billy? I didn't do anything wrong and neither did you!"

He leaned his head back on the couch and looked up at the ceiling. He closed his eyes for a moment to think. "Right now, we know nothing. We're gonna play dumb. Let me handle this. No matter what, and I mean this with everything in me, you do not say a word about what happened that night. Promise me, Mattie. Promise me."

Mattie started to protest but the look on Billy's face said otherwise. "I promise. But what if…"

Billy stopped her, "No what-ifs. Please, let me handle this."

The conversation was over. Mattie did not like the plan laid out before her.

*** * * ***

Lawson sat in the jail thinking over the Prewitt case. The evidence was leaning toward Billy Akers, but his gut was saying otherwise. He had learned over the years to listen to his gut. He wasn't sure if it was experience talking or the still, small voice of God guiding him. Either way, he trusted it. It had never steered him wrong. He needed to go to the Shearer place and check Billy's story about the pig he claimed to have given to Doris and Curtis. The jail was empty today. Soon it could be home to a murderer. Gene will have to dry out somewhere else.

As Sheriff Lawson rode to the Shearer homestead, two

plans were being finalized. Billy had convinced Matilda to stay silent, be cordial and cooperative, to play ignorant. Billy not only wanted to protect Mattie from the reputation and scandal of rape, he also wanted to protect them both from what the death of Frank might mean for their future. Dan and Charlie had decided that they would meet with their cousin and her husband, Elsie and Granville Creech, to develop a story for the sheriff. It needed to be simple, just enough to place suspicion on Billy Akers as an accessory to the murder. Joe Lawson had no idea what lay ahead. His belief in justice was about to be tested to its very core.

Curtis greeted Lawson as he rode up on Bullet, "Good mornin', sheriff. You're just in time. We have biscuits and gravy left if you'd like Doris to fix you a plate."

Joe didn't hesitate, "That sounds awfully good, Curtis. Don't mind if I do. I've got a couple of questions for you. We can discuss it while I fill my belly on Doris's delicious cooking."

They stepped inside and sat at the kitchen table while Doris warmed up breakfast.

"How are you feelin' Doris? You endured quite a scare, never seen anything like it."

Doris looked at Joe and shivered, "Oh, sheriff, I'll never forget that sight, not as long as I'm livin'."

Joe could tell that she was a long way from recovering from her gruesome discovery.

"I've been investigating, asking questions, and trying to piece together what happened. That's why I'm here actually. I was wondering, did Billy Akers happen to bring you two a slaughtered hog as payment? Did he bring it over here on that white ox of his?"

Curtis had decided on another plate of breakfast for himself as well, "Oh yeah he sure did. Some mighty good pork came off'n that hog. I helped him out and he wanted to pay me back. He's a fine young man that one is."

Joe thought for a moment, "Yes, yes he is. I was looking around their property, trying to figure out how Frank ended up there. I noticed some stains on their ox's side. When I asked him about it he told me that he had carried a hog he had slaughtered over here and that there must still be some blood stains from that on her. I just wanted to check it out and make sure that was true."

Curtis looked puzzled, "That's strange. As much rain as we had back in September, I would have thought she'd been completely cleaned off by now."

Joe was just about to take another bite of biscuit when his fork stopped just in front of his mouth, "September? When did he bring you the meat?"

Curtis didn't hesitate, "Oh that was near the end of August, I believe the 21st. I know because Doris's birthday is the 24th and she loves her some pork. That hog meant that she was going to have some for her birthday. I think that might have been the best present she'd ever received,"

Curtis and Doris both chuckled, "I do love pork," Doris chimed in.

Joe contemplated this information for a moment. If Billy brought a slaughtered hog to the Shearers in August, there is no way that the bloodstains from that would still show up on the ox's hide. September had been the wettest month they had seen in a long time. There's little doubt that all traces of Doris's birthday feast would have been gone by now. It had, however, been unusually dry this winter.

Joe laid his fork on his empty plate, "Doris, thank you for a mighty fine breakfast. I left the house early this morning and didn't even give myself time to eat. I think you might have just saved me from starvation."

Doris laughed as she took his plate, "I'm glad to have kept you from withering away."

Joe got up from the table, "Well, I've got plenty of work to do and a murder to solve. Thanks for your help. I'll be in touch." He said his goodbyes and headed out to Bullet. Joe rode back to town at a slow walk in order to give himself time to ponder this new information.

As Charles sat on the front porch with Granville and Elsie, Elsie was in deep thought as she listened to Charles's words, "We know Bob had something to do with Eli's death. He may have even been the one who did it. They have to pay for that."

Granville listened. The death of Elijah had hit them hard. He was a favorite nephew of Elsie's, her brother's only son. Elsie's brother had died of cholera when Elijah was little and the death of his only son had been extremely hard on her sister-in-law. She hadn't been the same since it happened. None of them had.

"This is what I think. When the news officially gets out about Frank's murder, I'm going to tell the sheriff that I saw Frank going to Billy's place. We need to keep it simple; we can build on it later."

"No."

Both men looked at Elsie with surprise. She had been silent throughout the entire discussion.

"I'll tell the sheriff. Hearing it from a woman will make it more credible. I will do it...for my brother and for Eli."

Her eyes remained fixed; she never looked at them nor did her tone or emotions seem to change. She had a look of determination. No doubt, vengeance weighed heavily on her mind. The men agreed that coming from Elsie, the story would have more impact. Charles headed home and the Caudill clan awaited their opportunity.

RED BLOOD, WHITE OX

# CHAPTER 8

Sheriff Lawson and Bullet found their way to Billy and Matilda's place, more by providence than plan. Joe didn't remember purposely leading his horse in that direction, yet, here they were. What guided him here made little difference. He had to ask Billy about his explanation regarding the bloodstain. It would be impossible for that stain to have been there since August. He left Bullet to graze while he walked up to the house and knocked on the door.

"Hello, sheriff, what can I do for you?" Mattie hoped her internal fears were hidden.

"Hello there, Mrs. Mattie. Is Billy around?"

"Yes, sir, he is. He's in his shed working. Would you like for me to fetch him for you?"

Joe glanced in the direction of the shed, "No, no, that won't be necessary. I can go knock on the door. Thank you, ma'am."

Mattie felt increasing panic, "Everything ok, sheriff?"

Joe turned around with a look of concern, "I sure hope so Mrs. Mattie. I sure hope so." He turned around and headed in the direction of Billy's shed.

Billy hadn't heard the sheriff outside. He had been lost in thought as he carved more animals for the Noah's Ark that he had hoped to give their first child. It had taken some time to be able to even look at them, but he decided that he would finish the project in hopes that there would be another baby in the future. The work had brought a sense of normalcy to their situation. For a moment he wasn't thinking about the sheriff, Frank Prewitt, or what had happened that fateful night. The knocking at the door gave him a jump.

"Billy, you in there? It's Sheriff Lawson."

Billy opened the door, "Hey sheriff, I didn't hear you come up. What can I do for you?"

Joe glanced inside and noticed what appeared to be a cradle, "I just needed some clarification on something. When did you take that hog over to the Shearers?"

Billy thought for a moment; he knew it had been over the summer. He was wishing that he had come up with a better excuse for the blood on Bessie's back, "That was a while ago, early fall I believe."

"I spoke with Curtis. He was thinking it was around August," Joe waited for Billy's reaction.

"Yeah, I think that was about right. I was thinking early September but I'm sure Curtis is correct."

Joe looked around the farm and up at the clouds; he was hoping wisdom would come down from above, "Seems strange that your ox would still have blood from that slaughter in August. Don't you think? I mean, September was an extremely wet month, as I recall."

Billy had no explanation. September had been the wettest month in years. He felt backed into a corner so he decided to play ignorant, "I don't know, sheriff. I think it would take a smarter man than me to figure that out."

"Just seems odd that the rains wouldn't have washed that off. I'm thinking there has to be another explanation."

Billy tried to remain calm. He knew he had to be careful, "It does seem odd I reckon, but Bessie does love to stay under those trees." They both looked over at Bessie grazing in the field nearby, contentedly eating grass underneath the large branches of the surrounding trees. Billy said a little prayer of thanks to God above.

"That she does," Joe acknowledged, "that she does." The possibility was there, although Joe knew there was something he was missing. He still had more questions than answers.

Mattie sat on the bed trembling when Billy walked in. He sat next to her and held her. He had no words of comfort; he was trembling, too. Meanwhile, Sheriff Lawson was arriving in town with Billy on his mind. The cradle in Billy's workshop haunted him.

Mattie was quieter these days. The love of her homestead, the love of the outdoors, all of the things that had brought her so much joy in the past, seemed to elude her. She tried to hide it from Billy. She no longer accompanied him hunting. Instead, she would stay behind and curl up in the bed for hours, often staring blankly ahead lost in her thoughts. There were times that she found herself spending most of the day in tears. She mourned her baby, she mourned her peace of mind, and she grieved for her sense of safety in this world. It was no longer a world full of beauty and adventure. It was now replaced with fear and loss. Life would never be the same. Rest rarely came to her, visions of Frank Prewitt's eyes on her, the ax, the blood, would jolt her awake. Mattie was exhausted.

Frank was buried in the Caudill cemetery. Few showed up for the funeral, Elsie and Granville, Dan, Charlie, and their wives. Sheriff Lawson attended with Marcus. Dan had sent a letter to Frank's sister about his death. She had replied that she had no interest in anything her brother had nor in handling any of the arrangements. Elsie chose the suit to bury him in. It was the cheapest one she could find. No one would be seeing it on him considering the state of his body. Regardless of the lack of affection for the man, if he did happen to make it to the pearly gates, one shouldn't find themselves naked. As Charles and Granville filled the grave with dirt, Dan discussed plans with Elsie.

"When do you plan on speaking with the sheriff?"

Elsie looked toward downtown, "I'll be heading into town next week for supplies. I'll make sure to run into Joe. Don't you worry." She laid the flowers that were meant for Frank's grave onto Eli's.

Billy walked into his parents' house as they were finishing up breakfast. He knew word had gotten around about Frank's body being found and he needed to get some advice and explain what happened. As Billy entered the kitchen, his mother turned around and placed her hands on her hips with defiance on her face. Before she could utter a word, Bob stopped her.

"Sarah, stop. I'll handle this."

Deflated by Bob's interference, she shot Billy a disapproving glare and went back to cleaning up.

"Let's go for a walk before your mama beats you with a spoon, boy."

Billy wasn't looking forward to this meeting, but he knew if anyone would know what to do it was his daddy.

"I'm hearing rumors that you have found yourself in a bit of trouble." Bob studied Billy as he spoke.

Billy took a deep breath, "They found Frank Prewitt's body on our place, Daddy. His head was cut off. The Shearers' dog dug up the head and Doris found it by their house. Just about scared her to death."

Bob looked down and a smirk found its way onto his face, "Now that's kinda funny, you have to admit," he continued to chuckle, "I bet Doris had a fit on that poor dog."

Billy grinned sheepishly. It was difficult for him to find the humor in it.

"Did you kill him?"

"No, sir. I did not."

Billy looked him straight in the eye and did not turn away. Bob believed him. "What happened then? Because, son, you are facing some trouble, if not with the law then with the Caudills."

Billy knew he found himself within a feud that he had successfully avoided until now, "You better sit down. This is a long story."

Billy began to tell him of the hunting trip and the scene that he came home to. That he found Frank dead and beheaded in the front room of their home with Mattie unconscious and beaten near the washbasin. How the injuries inflicted upon her had caused her to lose their baby. He admitted to his father that he hid the body with plans to bury it deeper when the ground had thawed. He could have never predicted that a dog would wander in that spot and dig up the head. Billy told him about the bloodstains found on Bessie and how the sheriff was asking a lot of questions. It all came out like flowing water and Billy felt lighter with every word he uttered. Bob sat quietly listening and pondering the situation. When Billy was finished, Bob said nothing for what felt like an eternity. Billy felt fidgety and nervous but knew he could not show it.

"So did Matilda kill him?"

"Yes sir, she did."

Bob shook his head in disbelief, "That is hard to imagine. Your wife is a tough one but to decapitate a man seems hard to imagine. How do you know?"

"She told me herself, sir. She had no memory of it for a while but when the sheriff came by and she had healed up some, she remembered it all. He did some horrible things to her. He deserved to die." Billy could feel the anger bubbling up inside of him. "I buried him with his head at his feet. It was the only thing I could do."

Bob looked at his son. He had never expected Billy to have that kind of anger, "Damn," Bob said quietly, "you were right to do that."

They sat under the trees and listened to the birds. A plan had to be made, Billy's future was at stake. "We can't avoid retribution from the Caudill clan. They will get their revenge, mark my words. They are still raw from the death of Elijah and have been looking for a way to avenge his death. The fact remains that you did not kill Frank Prewitt. You could tell Joe the truth. You could tell him about what Frank did to Matilda."

Billy straightened up, "No. Absolutely not. I won't make her a target for the Caudills and I will not allow Mattie to be the town gossip. They will judge her for what happened and whisper as she walks by. I won't let that happen. I'm the one who told Frank to stop by the house when I wasn't going to be there. I knew she didn't feel comfortable with him, but I did it anyway. What happened to her, to our baby, is on me. I should have been there. It's all my fault. I'll protect her till the end, Daddy."

Bob began calming his son down, "Ok, ok, calm down, I

get it. I do. If somebody did that to your mother, he'd be a dead man as sure as I'm standing. It's not your fault though, son. It's Frank Prewitt's fault. He's the one who made the decision to do that, nobody else. I guarantee the Caudills don't give a shit about Frank, but they need something to give them momentum to get back at us for Eli. If Eli's death wasn't in the mix, I doubt they would care." Bob closed his eyes to concentrate, "We need to come up with a story. Joe is a fair man. Let's go for a walk, walking helps me think."

Elsie had contemplated long and hard on how she was going to approach the sheriff. She decided that she would enlist the help of her young cousin, Melissa. Coming from Melissa, there would be less suspicion. Melissa could use Elsie as a witness, making the story more legitimate. Elsie spoke with Melissa, explaining that there was little doubt that Billy had a hand in Frank's death. Melissa was hesitant at first but finally agreed that an Akers had to pay for the death of Elijah. She and Elijah had grown up together and his death had hit her especially hard. It was like losing a brother. A plan was formed and Melissa decided to not waste any time acting. She was afraid that the longer she waited, the less likely she would be to see it through. She had figured out what days the sheriff was most likely to be in town. It seems that every Wednesday, he cleans the jail and goes by the store for supplies. She was going to ensure that she and Joe Lawson would run into each other at Mr. Hobbs's store.

Right on time, Sheriff Lawson walked through the doors of the store just as Melissa had started picking out some of her goods. She had planned well. She sauntered her way in his direction.

"Well, good afternoon, sheriff. How have you been?"

Joe turned around to see Melissa, "Oh, I've been fairly well, Miss Melissa. Thanks for asking. Awful busy these days, unfortunately."

Melissa didn't miss a beat, "Yes, I heard. Elsie told mama that they found Frank dead. Scary, really...to think someone could be so...violent!" She shivered for effect. "Seems like yesterday I just saw Frank, heading out to the Akers place to work on some boots. He couldn't fix Daddy's that day because of it. That was the last time I saw him. Daddy's boots are still a mess," she shook her head in disbelief.

Joe was curious, "Is that right? That is a shame. How long ago was that?"

Melissa thought a minute, "It was before Thanksgiving, in the fall. I remember the leaves were so pretty." She smiled her sweet smile. Joe smiled back. "It's been nice talking to you, sheriff. I hope things get better for you."

"Thank you, Miss Melissa. So do I." He looked absently at the dry beans and thought about the information he had just received. Melissa stated that the last time she saw Frank had been in the fall. What she did not realize is how close to the truth her lie actually was.

Billy walked through his door just as the sun was beginning to set. Mattie had already eaten but was keeping his dinner warm on the stove.

"How was your visit with your daddy?" She was dreading what had come from the meeting. She knew if anyone would be able to help them sort through this mess, it was her father-in-law.

"It went better than I expected. He knows everything. Why don't we talk about it after supper? I'm starving,"

Billy sat down to his meal. Matilda decided to go feed the chickens in order to allow Billy to eat in peace. He was carrying a heavy load in order to protect her, whether she wanted him to or not.

Billy had ravaged his supper and was sitting on the front porch when Mattie walked back to the house. She sat down in the rocking chair beside him and looked out at the sky painted with the colors of the day. They sat quietly for a long time when Billy began, "Frank's death is going to start trouble with the feud. It's unavoidable. Eli was killed in a confrontation last year and they have been looking for an open door to revenge. Frank offers it. That part we have to accept. We've decided that if pressured,

I will admit to hiding the body after finding it on the property. That I have no idea how he got there or who did it, but in order to protect my family, I buried it. The most I will get is a little jail time for hiding the body and the feud may not come knocking on our door. It will just flare up and die down again as it's been doing."

Mattie didn't like it, any of it, "Billy if I talk to the sheriff…"

"No! You are not going to be a chapter in this feud. Not only that, do you have any idea what life would be like for you if the folks in this town knew what happened?? Not only would you be the gossip of the town, but our kids would also have to hear about it, too. This is how it's going to be done, Mattie. I love you, I respect you, but I'm putting my foot down. Daddy agreed it was the best thing to do."

"But, Billy," Mattie felt the tears welling up inside of her, "what if they think you killed him. What if something happens to you?"

Billy looked straight ahead, "We're not going to think like that. But whatever happens, you stick to the plan…or…I'll never forgive you. I mean it. Promise me."

Mattie was stunned. Billy had never spoken to her like that before, "I promise." She looked out toward the darkening world that surrounded them, tears rolling down her cheeks.

※ ※ ※

The morning sun was rising over the horizon when Joe mounted his horse. The evidence was mounting and he didn't want to admit where all the signs were pointing. His gut kept telling him there was something he was missing but his mind couldn't deny that the more he discovered, the more guilty Billy Akers appeared. Unable to stomach his breakfast, he left it untouched on the table. He knew he would have company in the jail later.

Billy wasn't surprised to hear the hoof beats of the

sheriff's horse coming down the road. There was no avoiding the inevitable. It was best to look it straight in the eye. This was the first time that Billy had not felt panic or fear. He was completely at peace with whatever came next. As Joe got closer, Billy could see by the look on his face that things were going downhill. This was the moment of truth.

"Good mornin', sheriff. You're certainly out early this morning."

Joe dismounted and led Bullet to some grass to graze. "Hey, Billy. I had an interesting conversation yesterday and wanted to talk to you about it. Can we have a seat inside?"

Billy wanted Matilda as far away from this as possible. "Here let's go to my woodshed. This Frank Prewitt mess has Mattie pretty upset. I'd rather she be protected from it if you don't mind."

"Of course, of course, lead the way," Joe followed Billy to the little shed by the tree line. As they stepped inside, Joe immediately caught sight of the small crib and beautifully carved animals, "Billy, did you make these? This is some beautiful work. Is Mattie expecting?" He could see the sadness fall on Billy's shoulders.

"She was. She lost the baby. I'm saving these for the next one."

"I'm sorry. Sorry to hear that. Recently?"

Billy nodded, "Yes, sir, just before Christmas. It's hard for her to talk about. I don't want to upset her anymore with all of this going on. What can I help you with?"

Joe's heart sank, everything felt heavy. He knew he had to keep moving forward regardless of what his gut was telling him. "I was speaking to Melissa Elam at the store yesterday, sweet young lady. She was talking about hearing of Frank's death and such. Well, in that conversation, she mentioned that the last time she saw Frank he was walking toward your farm. Do you know anything about that?"

Billy looked at Joe without hesitation, "Yes, he used to do some work for me when my shoes needed mending. I'm pretty hard on boots. He was up here, not sure when, but I'm sure he came up to repair my shoes."

"Billy, I'm going to be honest with you. All evidence is pointing to you being the one who killed Frank Prewitt. I don't want to believe it myself but everything is pointing in that direction. I can't deny it. As much as I want to, I just can't. If you have anything you need to tell me, now is the time to do it."

Billy looked at him for a long time, then he looked out the little window of his shop. He could see Bessie grazing in the field, the chickens in their coop, the wilderness behind them. It all felt surreal. With a deep breath, he began, "I was out scouting. It was just before Christmas. I was just looking for some small game. Something caught my eye, looked out of place. When I got closer, it was Frank. His head had been cut off. It was awful. I didn't know what to do. I knew he was a Caudill and I knew this didn't look good for me. So, I got Bessie; I packed him up, and I buried him. I panicked. I just wanted the whole thing gone. I've never wanted to be a part of this feud, sheriff. With Frank being on my property, I knew I would be pulled in. I couldn't have that for me, Mattie, and definitely the baby."

Joe was watching him the whole time he spoke. He believed him, or maybe he just wanted to. It's hard to say. "Billy, I appreciate your honesty. I still have to take you in. You understand, don't you? You hid a murder and I can't just pretend that didn't happen. It's my job, Billy. It's what I'm sworn to do."

Billy nodded in understanding, "Would you give me a minute to go talk to Mattie? I need to reassure her."

"Absolutely," Joe agreed, "I'm in no hurry. I'll wait over here with Bullet."

With that, Billy walked slowly to the house. Mattie was sitting on the edge of the bed, she knew what was coming.

"I'm going with Joe, Mattie. It'll be alright." Billy was hoping his words were prophetic and not just wishful thinking.

Mattie didn't move. She was looking down at her hands, "If I told the sheriff what happened Billy…"

Billy stopped her immediately, "Mattie, you promised me.

You have to stick to the plan. He is arresting me because I hid the body, that's it. I may have to spend some time in jail, but then this whole thing can be behind us. Daddy said if you need anything to let him know. I'm going to send word to him about what has happened and he will be checking in on you. It's going to be ok. Promise me you'll stick to the plan."

Mattie was terrified. Deep within her soul, she knew this wasn't going to work out as they thought. The idea of living under Billy's unforgiveness was almost unbearable. She felt completely torn, but Billy was staring down at her waiting for an answer and Sheriff Lawson was waiting for him to come back out.

"I promise, Billy. I promise."

She looked up at him and Billy's heart broke as he saw the tears welling up in her eyes. There had to be an end to all of this pain.

"I love you, Mattie. Know that." He sat beside her and held her in his arms as she wept. Gently placing his hands on her cheeks, he turned her face toward him giving her a knowing smile of reassurance, "I love you." Kissing her softly on the forehead he assured her, "I'll be back soon." He gently kissed her lips and got up to face the inevitable.

As they rode down the dirt road away from the Akers homestead, Mattie stepped out on the porch. "I love you, Billy," she whispered to herself. She felt to blame for all that was happening.

The jail door slammed behind Billy, the reality of the situation weighing heavy on him. The what-ifs began creeping into his mind. What he knew was that he did not kill Frank Prewitt, he also knew that Prewitt deserved to die. One thing was for certain, a murder charge equaled a town square hanging. Billy tried to shake the thought out of his head.

"Sheriff, would you mind sending word to Daddy that I'm here?"

As Sheriff Lawson looked at Billy in the cell, he knew in his gut that something was wrong in all of this, "Sure, Billy, I was planning on heading up there this afternoon."

Billy nodded, "Thank you kindly." He sat down to think. There was nothing else he could do.

It was a beautiful clear day. The ride to Bob's place along with the serenity of the scenery allowed Joe to think. Why would Billy admit to burying Frank if he had killed him? Who would have wanted to kill Frank? He contemplated these things as he and Bullet rode on. He couldn't shake the image of the baby cradle.

Bob saw the sheriff ride up, he knew what had happened. He met him halfway, "Good afternoon, sheriff. What can I do for you?"

Joe pulled the reins to bring Bullet to a stop and hopped off, "I need to talk to you, Bob. It's about Billy."

Bob cocked his head, "He ain't hurt is he?" He knew the truth and hoped Sheriff Lawson didn't realize that.

"No, Bob. Billy is in jail. I've had to arrest him. He's charged right now with hiding the body of Frank Prewitt and not reporting it. I'm gonna be honest, Bob, the evidence is pointing at Billy as the murderer. It's hard for me to believe that, but evidence is evidence, Bob. Do you know anything about Frank's murder? Your boy could hang."

Bob looked behind him. Sarah was standing on the front porch watching. If anything happens to Billy, it would break her heart. "Let's walk up the road, sheriff. This kind of talk will upset Sarah."

They began walking back down the dirt road, "I'm not sure how Frank ended up dead," Bob began, "but I know Billy didn't do it. He's not capable. Normally, I would think it was a feud killing, but I haven't gotten wind of anything. Billy probably thought the same when he found Frank and was just protecting his family. He's a good man. He's not like me, sheriff. I don't know who killed Frank, but it wasn't Billy. That I know."

Joe stood quiet looking out at the day surrounding him, "I believe you, Bob. I do. I just hope I can find some evidence to prove it. We have witnesses saying they saw Frank headed to

Billy's place. It doesn't look good."

Bob shot a look of anger at Joe, "Frank was a cobbler. Hell yeah, he probably went to Billy's. Billy used him to repair his shoes. Anybody who says otherwise is a liar and probably a Caudill!"

Joe knew he was probably right, "The witnesses were women, Bob. I'm not saying I think Billy killed him. I'm saying the evidence is pointing that way. I just wanted to let you know what's going on and that I'm holding him at the jail. Matilda is home alone. You might want to check on her or let her family know. Billy said she had lost a baby a while back. Mighty sad. This is a lot on her. I'll keep you posted." And with that, Joe mounted his horse and headed back to town.

Bob stood and watched him leave. Dark days were coming.

Matilda sat on the porch staring out into her world. The birds continued their song, the sun continued to move across the sky, the breezes continued to blow, yet for her, everything had stopped. She felt nothing; she heard nothing. She only vaguely noticed the sounds of a horse slowly approaching her home.

"I knew you would come," she said without making eye contact.

Bob dismounted his horse, "How you doing there, Mattie?"

He was concerned. Matilda may be sitting right in front of him, but she was obviously far away.

"He's gone," is all she could say.

"I know. I know, Mattie. But what I also know is sitting here staring at the trees ain't gonna change that. There's a time for mournin', but then we have to pick ourselves up and start fightin'. If we give up on the future, we give up on Billy."

Mattie turned to look at him. There were no tears, there was no rage, there was complete understanding. "What do I need to do? Tell me and I'll do it."

Bob's face softened, it was a look that Mattie had never seen. He was a man full of himself, bubbling over. Right now, he was a man concerned for his son with immense compassion for his son's beloved.

"All I need you to do is be there for Billy. That's it. Give him hope. Don't, and I mean don't ever, give up. Can you do that?"

Mattie's gaze did not falter, "Yes, sir."

Bob shook his head knowingly, "You do that. I'll take care of the rest."

# CHAPTER 9

Mattie worked hard. Farm duties did not stop for a crisis. She had been able to gather enough apples for a pie, Billy's favorite. She hoped that something fresh from home might lift his spirits. Peeling the apples, she began to sing to herself, *"Draw me nearer...nearer blessed Lord, to the cross where thou hast died."* A knot formed in her throat and her lip began to quiver. She hummed the remainder of the hymn as she continued her labor of love. Bob's visit had brought her a sense of peace and purpose, but the loneliness for Billy and the gravity of the situation still weighed heavily upon her. She prayed nightly for a miracle.

Mattie rode into town to visit Billy. The pie was cooling as she pulled up to hitch her horse. Carefully carrying the pie, she walked in the direction of the jail, passing Elsie Creech on the way.

"Good afternoon, Mrs. Creech."

"Good afternoon." Elsie turned as she passed, watching Mattie take her gift of love to her husband. For a moment, she thought she felt a twinge of guilt. She quickly replaced it with the face of Elijah and continued toward Mr. Hobbs's store.

"Sorry, Mattie, strictly business," she whispered to herself.

Joe looked up as he heard the door open. "Good afternoon, Mrs. Mattie. What do we have here?"

"Hello, sheriff. I baked Billy his favorite dessert, apple pie. There's plenty to share if you'd like a slice."

"Don't mind if I do, ma'am. That sounds delicious."

Mattie sat the pie down and began preparing a slice for each of them. Sheriff Lawson inspected everything dutifully, then quickly devoured his slice.

"Thank you, Mrs. Mattie. That was amazing. I will sit outside and allow you and Billy some privacy. You have an hour."

Joe stepped out leaving Mattie and Billy alone. Billy reached for his wife's hand, "How are you doing, sweetheart? I've been worried sick about you out there all by yourself."

"I'm doing ok, Billy. I just miss you something awful. It's so quiet there now. Sometimes it brings me peace, but most of the time, it's painfully lonely."

"I know, this will all be over soon. Just have faith."

"I have been trying. I won't lie to you, it's difficult. But there's something else; I might be expecting." She looked at him with hope. It was a hope clouded in uncertainty.

"Are you serious? Do you know for sure?" Billy was shocked.

"No. I'm not sure, but I suspect I am. I haven't had my flow for a few weeks."

"Oh, Mattie! I wish I could hug you right now! This will keep me going while I'm locked up in this cage!" He squeezed her hand tight.

Joe sat on the bench outside the jail and watched the townspeople pass by. Elsie Creech was approaching.

"Hello, sheriff. Beautiful day today isn't it?"

"Yes ma'am it is. Nasty storm the other night. Did y'all have any problems out at your place?"

"No, no...everything was fine. Praise the Lord. I hear you have a new tenant these days."

"Yes, it appears as such."

"Quite a shame, isn't it? Hard to believe, really. Billy has always been so quiet. Last time I saw Frank I only got to speak to him for a minute. He said Billy Akers had all kinds of work for him to do. Had been keeping him awfully busy he said." Elsie shook her head in disbelief, "Makes you wonder what sets a person off, doesn't it?"

"I suppose. When did you last speak to Frank?" Joe's curiosity was piqued.

"End of October, during the Harvest Celebration. He had

been drinking a little nip. I do hate how the men love to get into the moonshine at those gatherings."

"Yes ma'am, I always have a few overnighters with me that night," Joe chuckled. "It was nice seeing you, Mrs. Elsie. Tell Granville hello for me, please." He tipped his hat and considered this new information.

"Good day to you, sheriff. I most certainly will." Elsie walked away; a look of defiance on her face.

Joe knew he had to go back to the Akers farm and look around. He would wait until Mattie left, giving her time to get home. Then he would ride out and talk to her alone. Mattie stepped out the door.

"I left the rest of that pie on your desk, sheriff. You and Billy can have another slice after supper."

"Thank you, ma'am. I'll try to remember to share it with Billy." He smiled, although inside a feeling of sadness lay heavy on him. Mattie returned the smile, boarded her wagon, and rode home.

Billy sat alone in his cell. He was smiling as the news that Mattie just shared floated around in his head. He couldn't wait to get home to his family.

Mattie was working in the garden later that afternoon when Sheriff Lawson rode up. "Everything ok? Is Billy alright?"

"Yes ma'am, Billy is fine. I was hoping to talk to you if I could. Could we go inside and sit down?"

"Absolutely, sheriff. Come right in."

They walked into the house and had a seat in the front room. With a deep breath, Joe began, "I've had someone else tell me that they talked to Frank and that he was coming to see Billy. These reports all state that it was in the late fall which would correlate with about the time that Frank was killed. Mattie, that doesn't fair well for Billy. I have to be honest. If there is anything you can tell me to clear his name, now is the time. I'm beginning to think he did more than just hide Frank's body."

Mattie felt numb. "I really don't understand why so many people are talking about Billy and Frank. Billy didn't use his services any more than the other men around here." She was agitated and suspicious that this was the work of the Caudill clan.

"I truly am hoping it is merely a coincidence." Joe looked down. Again, he noticed the replacement boards used on the floor, "Looks like you had some floor issues here."

Mattie knew the boards were replaced while she was unconscious. She also knew why. "Yes, sir. A house is always needing repairs."

"That is very true, Mrs. Mattie. No doubt about that." Joe began looking behind the chair.

"Is there something wrong, sheriff?" Mattie had no idea what Sheriff Lawson had found. She tried not to panic.

"Not sure...there's a weird stain on this wall. Wanted to make sure it isn't something else that needs to be repaired for you. If so, I could give you a hand." Joe wanted to investigate further without revealing his suspicions.

"Oh, it's fine sheriff. I'm sure of it. No need to worry yourself. I'm quite capable of taking care of it, whatever it is."

Joe moved the chair and studied it. The stain was brownish in color. He rubbed his finger across and scratched it. It began flaking.

"That looks like blood."

Mattie felt a surge of fear. She sat speechless staring at the sheriff. She needed to tell him the truth. She needed to clear Billy. What would happen to her? To the baby?

"Sheriff may I ask you why you are rearranging my son's furniture?!" Mattie jumped at the sound of Bob's voice. He was standing in the doorway. She had been so consumed by Sheriff Lawson's discovery, she hadn't heard him walk in. Relief washed over her.

"Bob it's not a good idea to sneak up on a lawman with a gun! It's a good way to get shot if you want to know the truth."

"Why are you here, sheriff? Why are you snooping around? Don't you think Mattie has enough on her mind without you harassing her?"

"Bob I have every right to be here. I am investigating a

murder and I am going to find out what happened. There are bloodstains on this wall and I need to know where they came from."

"Look around you, sheriff!" Bob was agitated. "This is a farm. There's blood everywhere, chickens, pigs, deer, rabbits. Doesn't mean its Frank's blood! I think you need to be heading back to the jail." He stood defiantly, staring down Sheriff Lawson.

"I'll be checking back with you, Mrs. Mattie. Thank you again for the pie. Bob, it would serve your son well to not get in the way of this investigation."

"It would serve you well, sheriff, to go find the actual killer and quit trying to frame my son."

Joe was visibly frustrated. He decided that leaving the Akers farm and coming back when he did not have to argue with Bob would be the better choice. He let himself out and rode back to town.

"You ok?" Bob's attention turned to Mattie.

"Yes, sir. I was about to tell him. I was about to break my promise. This has to stop. It just has to!" She was beginning to break.

"Listen to me, Mattie. What did we decide? We are in this together. Do you understand?"

Mattie nodded in agreement, "I might be with child. I told Billy today."

Bob stared blankly for a moment, "What do you think would have happened to the baby if you had confessed everything? You have got to stick to the plan Mattie, for Billy, for the baby, and for you, too"

"I didn't do anything wrong! Frank did! I'm tired of lying about it!"

Bob understood her frustration. "I know. I know you didn't. You have to think beyond that. If you tell Lawson about what Frank did to you, the whole town will know. They may or may not believe you. You will live with whispers for the rest of your life. When that baby goes to school, they will know about his mama who was raped by the cobbler. Do you want that?"

"No, sir. I want Billy out of jail. I want this whole mess behind us."

"Then let me handle it. Please."

Mattie agreed. She knew she had to protect the baby.

"We have some family in Virginia. I want to send you there while this is going on." Mattie began to protest. "Mattie, this is for your protection. Joe will be back in the next day or two. It's too much stress. Billy would never forgive me if I let anything happen to you or that little calf you're carrying." Bob grinned at Mattie.

Mattie grinned back although she was not happy about the idea of not only leaving town but leaving the state. She rubbed her hand across her belly. This all seemed so unfair. She knew that if the sheriff pressured her again, she would break. What would happen then? What if they didn't believe her? What if she lost the baby?

"Ok. I'll go. When should I leave?"

"Tomorrow morning. I will be by to pick you up and take you to the coach in Owsley County. That way we can avoid Sheriff Lawson. I'll take care of the farm while you are gone. I'll explain everything to Billy. Send your letters to me and I will make sure that he gets them. See you in the mornin', ok?"

"See you in the morning. Thank you." She hugged her father-in-law and for the first time, felt a kinship with him.

Mattie collected a few belongings and made ready for her trip. She climbed into bed, exhausted by the day's events. Sleep, however, would not come to comfort her.

❋ ❋ ❋

Elsie Creech lay in her bed, staring at the ceiling. The image of Matilda Akers could not be shaken. She had always liked Matilda and considered her to be a good woman, a hard-working one. Matilda chose to marry an Akers. That was on her.

The more Elsie tried to justify her actions the deeper the image of Matilda innocently delivering the pie to her husband burned into her brain. This feud brought out the devil in all involved. She said a prayer as Granville slept peacefully beside her.

"Dear Lord, I would never ask for forgiveness for what I have done to Billy Akers. I know that forgiveness leads to repentance and I have no intention of taking back what I did. But I do ask you to forgive me for what I am doing to Matilda. She had no idea what she was doing when she married an Akers. She was blinded by love, Lord, and I hate that my actions will hurt her. You say vengeance is yours Father, but I can't wait for you to act. Elijah didn't deserve to die, but an Akers does. May you have mercy on my soul. Amen."

As the hills of Clay County slept, two women lay awake and considered their fates till the early morning light.

# CHAPTER 10

Mattie was in Billy's woodshop before daylight. There were a few items of importance that she wanted to keep safe while she was in Virginia. She knew Billy had a hiding place in the floorboards of the shop. He had no idea that she knew where it was. She found it quite by accident when she was looking for a tool she needed. Billy had been away on a hunting trip at the time. There was nothing in it then, but she knew that was where he liked to hide his presents to her. She entered the small building and set the lantern on a table. Carefully loosening the board, she removed it and set it to the side. It was difficult to see in the low light. She could see enough to realize the space wasn't empty. She brought the lantern closer. Inside, there was a collection of small carved animals. She picked them up one by one and looked at them, two giraffes, two elephants, and others. Two by two, just like Noah's Ark.

"Oh, Billy."

Her heart was full of love. She knew he had made these for the baby they lost. She decided that she would take one of the animals with her to Virginia. It made her feel close to her husband. Placing a small giraffe to the side, she filled the space with her things and the cared animals placing the board back as it was. She inspected the area to make sure it was inconspicuous. She was impressed at what an amazing woodworker her husband was. The world was getting lighter. Time was running short.

She went inside to make sure everything was in order and that she had not forgotten to pack anything. She carried her bag to the front porch and set it down. Before her father-in-law arrived, she had one more thing she must do. Mattie walked toward the pen that held the great white ox, Bessie. Mattie went inside and approached her. As she stood beside her, she gently stroked her strong neck.

"Thank you, ol' girl. You never ask questions, do you? You just do your job for us because you trust us. For that, I am eternally grateful. You are a wonderful friend. Take care while I am away. Bob will be taking care of you. Don't take any foolishness off of him, ya hear?"

She smiled at the animal and gave her a couple more good pats. Bessie stood contentedly chewing her cud. Mattie made her way back to the porch to await her ride. She could hear a wagon in the distance.

* * *

Joe finished his breakfast and gathered his things. Giving his wife a kiss he prepared her for another long day. "It may be a long one today, Agnes. Don't worry about keeping supper warm." Agnes returned his kiss and smiled. She was used to his job taking him away. It was part of being married to a lawman.

The sheriff mounted Bullet and headed toward the Akers farm. He wanted to get there as early as possible. As the little cabin came into view, all seemed quiet. Joe let Bullet graze while he approached the house. He knocked on the door but there was no answer. He tried a second time and called out.

"Mrs. Mattie? Are you home? It's Sheriff Lawson, I'd like to ask you a few questions."

Still, there was nothing.

Joe opened the door and entered, "Mrs. Mattie?" The house was silent. He went back out and checked the buildings, barns, and coops. There was no one to be found. Going back into the house, Joe decided this would be the perfect time to investigate the stain he saw on the wall earlier. Not surprisingly, he found the stain had been removed.

"Dammit."

He continued to look at the wall when something caught his eye. Small dots speckled the upper third of the wall. Using a chair, he stepped up for a closer look. It was blood. Standing there, he looked down at the floorboards recently replaced directly below him. The ax beckoned him from across the floor. Lawson was beginning to see what happened. Frank had been decapitated in the area that those boards had been replaced using the ax located within easy reach. The force necessary would easily cause the blood splatter to reach the upper wall. Joe knew there was only one thing left to do.

❋ ❋ ❋

Melissa Elam sat at the kitchen table talking with Elsie as she poured them both a cup of coffee. "I can't do it, Elsie. I haven't slept since I talked to the sheriff. Billy didn't kill nobody; we both know that."

Elsie set a cup in front of Melissa and sat down. She took a sip out of her own cup with no reaction. "Melissa, we are in a feud. That's as good as a war around here. Sometimes we have to do things that we aren't proud of. What you need to do is focus less on the deed and more on the reason."

"It's wrong. It's just wrong." Melissa was visibly distraught. "I can't keep this in anymore. It will kill me!"

Elsie set her cup down and stared at Melissa. "So, what are you going to do? Go tell the sheriff the truth? Get us all in trouble? For who? Billy Akers?! Do you have any idea how many of our family have died at the hands of the Akers? I can tell you this. Behind every killing, Bob Akers had something to do with it. Think of Billy as a sacrifice. That's how we get to the Akers. We sacrifice Billy but maybe we save countless others. The Bible tells of God asking Abraham to sacrifice his own son Isaac. Abraham didn't hesitate."

"But God delivered Isaac and provided a ram," Melissa

wasn't going to be deterred by her cousin's biblical references.

"That he did." Elsie looked straight ahead. "I suppose you could tell Joe the truth. But then, wouldn't we need a ram?" She turned and looked coldly at Melissa. Melissa felt the chill. She understood the implication.

"I suppose...if I'm saving the lives of family...God will forgive me." She tried to hide her sudden fear, but the stammering gave her away.

"I suppose he will." Elsie took another sip of her coffee and said no more.

* * *

Joe walked into the jail. Billy was sitting in his cell staring out at the morning sky. "Billy, I just came from your house. I found more bloodstains in your house. I have no choice. I am charging you with the murder of Frank Prewitt."

Billy continued to watch the clouds pass.

* * *

It took two days for Mattie to reach the station in Virginia. She was met by Ella Brewer, a cousin to Billy on his mother's side. "Hello, you must be Mattie. It's nice to finally meet you. I do wish it were under better circumstances. My wagon is hitched right over here."

Thank you, Mrs. Ella. I appreciate you letting me stay with you. Bob thought it best."

"Oh, it's no problem at all. I'll enjoy the company." They walked to the back of the wagon and placed the few things that Mattie brought in the back. When we get to the house, you can change into some fresh clothes. You'll feel like a new woman and I can soak your dress. These coaches can get so dirty. It appears you may have sat in a dirty seat."

Mattie was relieved that she had nowhere else to be in a

dirty dress. She also wondered how long she had been walking around like that. They arrived at the Brewer home place. It was a beautiful piece of land surrounded by hills, just like back home. They unloaded her things and Ella showed her to her room.

"This is where you'll stay. The bed is comfortable and there's a nice breeze in the evenings through these windows. I think you'll like it." She smiled at Mattie, "Don't forget to get that dress to me so I can soak it. It's too pretty to be ruined."

"Yes, ma'am, I will. Thank you." Mattie sat on the edge of the bed. Her room was cozy. Ella was wonderful and comforting. Still, Mattie couldn't help but feel empty. Ella was right, maybe some fresh clothes and a good meal would lift her spirits. She picked out a new dress and began to change. Looking at her soiled dress she noticed the stain wasn't dirt at all. It was blood.

# CHAPTER 11

Mattie's heart sank. Her flow had started. She wasn't pregnant. The idea that she was finally carrying their long-awaited baby was what had kept her going. She knew that it was what kept Billy going too. He would be devastated. She couldn't tell him. Mattie had never hidden anything from Billy but this was different. When this was all over, they could try again.

In order to hide her secret, she needed to hide it from Ella. With a closer look at the stain, she would know that it was blood. There was little doubt that Ella would tell Sarah and then word would get to Billy. Mattie had to soak the dress herself. There was no time to mourn.

Mattie finished getting dressed and began putting her things away. The small, wooden giraffe fell onto the floor. Picking it up, Mattie felt the comfort of it in her hand. Tears were fighting their way out, but she couldn't allow it. She placed the giraffe by her bedside and collected her soiled dress.

"Mrs. Ella, I'm going to go ahead and soak this dress myself. There's no telling what was on that coach seat. Billy's mama gave me a surefire stain removal remedy if you could just direct me to where you keep your soft soap, some powdered starch, and salt; I'll get right on it."

"Of course his mama gave you a surefire remedy. Who do you think taught her?" Ella smiled at Mattie, "I don't mind at all to do it for you so you can rest."

"I'm fine, Mrs. Ella. I've been cooped up in that coach for two days. It will feel good to be doing something."

"Well, if you insist. And please, just call me Ella. We're family."

"Thank you, Ella. Much obliged."

Mattie gathered her supplies and poured the water that Ella had been warming into a tub. As she scrubbed, she watched as the stain slowly disappeared from the dress. While the blood slowly faded away, so too did her hope.

Billy stared at the late morning sky. He heard the words come from Sheriff Lawson's lips, but couldn't take his eyes off of the sunlight streaming in. He was going to be a father. God would not bring him such wonderful news if He wasn't going to deliver him from this.

"That's fine, sheriff. Do what you have to do. I know I am innocent and so does the good Lord."

Joe was taken aback by Billy's lack of reaction. "You could hang for this Billy. You do know that?"

"Yes sir. I know that a man who murders another man will hang for it. But I never murdered Frank Prewitt, so I'm not going anywhere but back home."

Billy's confidence left Sheriff Lawson unsettled. He had never seen a man so sincerely deny the accusations against him. Lawson couldn't deny the evidence. He had to allow logic to be in charge and not let his heart cause him doubt.

"Suit yourself, Billy. I'll send word to your daddy and Mattie…"

"Not Mattie. If you could please provide me with some paper and a pencil, I would like to tell her myself. If you don't mind, sir?"

"I suppose that will be fine. I will get those to you when I get back."

"Thank you." Billy laid down on his cot and continued to stare out the window.

Ella prepared a delicious meal of fried grouse with tomatoes and cucumbers. Even through her disappointment, Mattie had managed to clean her plate. She was embarrassed to ask for seconds, but Ella would have none of it. "Young lady there is plenty left, help yourself to some more. You are eating for two I hear."

"Thank you, ma'am. I don't mind if I do." She felt guilty for her lie, but it was unavoidable. She couldn't stand the thought of Billy's heart being broken yet again. After finishing her meal, Mattie excused herself to take a walk.

"That was delicious Mrs., sorry...I mean, that was delicious, Ella. Thank you so much. I'll help you clean up and then I will take a walk. It's such a beautiful day."

"No, you will not. You go ahead and go for your walk. I can take care of this. You've had a long trip, not to mention what you and Billy have been through. Go on, I won't take no for an answer."

Mattie smiled and thanked her again. She was relieved to be by herself for a moment and digest everything that was happening. A nearby path called out to her. Mattie walked it slowly, enjoying the beauty of the day. She admired the finches as they flew amongst the wildflowers. She could hear a woodpecker close by. Squirrels were jumping along the trees while a soft breeze was blowing. Continuing down the path, she could hear a creek nearby. The peaceful sound of the water beckoned her. A nearby boulder made for the perfect seat. Sitting by the creek, she felt the warmth of the sun and the cool breeze lifting her hair. She closed her eyes and wondered if Billy could feel that same breeze. It made her feel close to him to imagine that he could. She had hoped to find some time alone and cry. She sat and listened to the creek flow beside her. No tears came.

*June 15, 1849*

*My Dearest Matilda,*

*Thoughts of you have never left my mind. I imagine the day when I am out of this jail and back on the farm with you and the baby. To hold you again. To smell the woods and fresh air from our front porch. To hear the cries and laughter of our baby. Those are the thoughts that make the long days here bearable. Daddy has promised me that these letters will get to you. I hope that when you receive them, you can feel my love in every word.*

*I am not sure how to tell you this because I do not want you to worry.*

*Sheriff Lawson has charged me with the murder of Frank Prewitt. I am not scared and I do not want you to be. The good Lord knows the truth and he will deliver us from this. You have to believe it because I believe it and the good book says, where two or more gather in His name there He will be also. The only thing you need to worry about is taking care of yourself and the baby growing inside of you. Ella will feed you plenty, believe me. I love you my darling and cannot wait to see you again.*

*With all of my love,*

*Billy*

The charges against Billy Akers caused quite a stir in town. Dan walked through Charles' front door to see if he had heard the news. It appeared fate was working in their favor.

"We need to get to one of the jurors. We should know by the end of the week who will be on the jury. I suggest we pool our money together for bargaining." Dan had spent his walk to Charles and Esther's scheming.

"We have a little bit put back. We can probably get the Elam's to put in. What about you, Dan?"

"I've got a little put back myself. If we put it all together and steer one juror in our favor, we can control this case."

"I have some money." Esther had been listening by the door.

"Woman, how do you have money I don't know about?" Charles was visibly shocked.

"I don't tell you everything. I sold some quilts last winter and took the money and put it away. Just in case you decided to waste it on moonshine again!"

Charles was quiet. He was just a little bit afraid of Esther though he would never admit it. "That should get us something to work with. Do you want to talk to the Elams, Dan?"

"Yes, I'll go over there today. I want to know what we have to work with. We will need to get started the second we know who is serving on the jury."

Mattie received Billy's letter. Her heart sank as she read

the news of his murder charges. She sat on her bed and read it over again. Ella walked by and saw her.

"Everything ok?"

"No ma'am. They're charging Billy with murder. I don't know what I'm going to do. I have to get back there and tell them what happened. Billy didn't kill him! He didn't!"

"Shh, shh, shh child, listen to me. Are you listenin'? Bob is handling this, ok? I have strict instructions to keep you here where you are safe and to make sure you and the baby are taken care of. Bob told me that you made a promise to Billy. Do you remember that?"

"Yes, ma'am."

"Ok then. You need to have a little faith. If not in Bob, then at least in the Father above. Can you do that? For Billy?"

Mattie felt lost. She was beginning to feel imprisoned herself. This all seemed so complicated.

"Yes, ma'am. I can do that."

"Good, good. Now, if you need me, I will be outside gathering some vegetables from the garden. You can come join me if you like."

"I will in just a minute. I want to write Billy back, if that's ok?"

"Yes, that's fine, just fine." She patted Mattie's leg and stepped outside.

*July 25, 1849*

*My Dearest Husband,*

*I have read your words a hundred times and will read them a hundred times more. I am torn between the love you send and the desperation I feel. Being away from you is torture. Knowing you sit in that jail accused of the murder of a man who did not deserve to live on this earth is more than I can take. The only strength I find is in knowing that your faith is strong and that we will be reunited again. I dream of you daily. I dream of lying safe and warm in your arms. I dream of our children running through the woods in the sunshine. These dreams will be ours, my love. You give me the strength to believe it is so. I love you, my dear Billy. Please take care until I see you again.*

*With all my love,*

*Matilda*

Dan arrived home that evening with the money he had collected. After adding his own savings, there was a total of $35. With that amount, he might be able to steer two jurors. It all depended on who was picked to serve. He placed the money in a jar and put it away. Everything was coming together as planned.

# CHAPTER 12

Bob sat on his front porch thoughtfully smoking his pipe with his cousin, Leroy. There was no doubt that the Caudills were planning on framing Billy for the murder of Frank Prewitt. They needed to get ahead of the situation before it got out of hand.

"You know, Leroy, I've been pondering this…trying to get into the Caudill clan's head. I've had to really think about how I would handle this if I were in their position. The best thing that I could come up with is paying off a juror. They've already used their women folk to place Billy in suspicion. They have no pull with the judge or with Joe. The only avenue they have left is the jury. Sad part is, they have the money to do it." He took another long draw from his pipe.

"They don't have all that much money, do they? The Caudills aren't rich folks. How much do you think they could come up with?"

They're not rich, Leroy. You're right about that. But, they are good with money and with their hands. They're good farmers and carpenters. The women are excellent at sewing. They are able to bring in income in different ways. I hate to say it, but they are a talented bunch of hooligans. No doubt they have some cash socked away. The only wasteful one is that old Charlie with his moonshine…I'd say Esther has a handle on that. She's a mean ol' woman."

"How are we going to stop them, Bob? We have no idea who they might pay off. Ain't nobody going to admit to that."

"This is what I know. If I were going to pay off a juror, I'd choose the weakest one. The one who needs it most. A desperate man will forget his morals for survival. We'll know who is on the jury in a few days. We'll have to figure out which ones are the most desperate."

Leroy nodded in agreement. They sat in silence on the porch, looking out at the passing day. The summer was nearing its end.

Almost 4 months had passed since Mattie first arrived in Virginia. Although her time with Ella had been pleasant, Mattie was getting antsy to get back to Kentucky. It wouldn't be long before Ella would figure out that she was not with child. She wrote a letter to her daddy in hopes that he could send for her. She had only brought a small amount of money and Mattie felt obliged to cover her own expenses. What remained was not enough to cover travel from Virginia to her parent's farm. Her plan was to leave as soon as she received the last correspondence from Billy. Daddy sent her money for a coach back home. Two days later, Billy's letter came.

*September 12, 1849*

*My Dearest Matilda,*

*I think of you night and day. You and the baby never leave my mind. We will be together again and this nightmare will be behind us. Daddy stopped by and told me that mama is sick and has been for some time. He is not sure if she will pull out of it. It breaks my heart to not be able to see her. All I can do is pray that she will pull out of it and I can visit when all of this is over. This got me to thinking though, my love. Have you thought about names for the baby? I was hoping we could name the baby Sarah after mama if it is a girl. If it is a boy, I would like to name him after your grandfather, Ambrose. He was a good man and I would like our son to follow in that path as opposed to the one my family has chosen with this feud. So many have been hurt and many others have lost their lives. I pray if we have a son, he never gets mixed up in this foolishness.*

*The jury selection has been made. I do not know yet who is on the jury, but Joe says that it is a collection of mighty fine folks. He assures me that I should receive a fair trial. If that's the case, I hope to be home by Christmas.*

*I love you and I love Sarah or Ambrose. I love you all.*

*With all my love,*

*Billy*

Mattie's heart sank. It hurt her deeply to know that she was living a lie. She could not bring herself to tell Billy the truth. The idea of their growing family is what gave him hope and Mattie refused to take that away from him. She would respond to his letter when she got settled at her mama and daddy's. She would tell him that she was homesick and needed to be with family. She decided to leave in two days when Ella would go to her sister's. She went every Wednesday to visit. Usually, Mattie accompanied her, but this week she would excuse herself due to morning sickness. She seemed to be lying a lot these days.

Wednesday morning, Ella called for Mattie. "Mattie! I'm getting ready to go to Grace's! Are you ready?"

"Ella, if you don't mind, I'm going to stay here. This morning sickness has me down. I guess it's a good sign of the baby growing, but I'm afraid I won't be much company. I'd like to lie here and rest...if that's ok?"

"Well bless your heart. Should I stay here you think? I hate leaving you alone like this."

"No ma'am. Absolutely not. It will pass and I will be ok. It's just hitting me harder this morning. I will join you next week." Mattie shuddered at yet another lie.

"Alright, if you insist. You're sure you will be ok?"

Mattie nodded. "Yes ma'am. Now if you will excuse me, I'm going to lie down and rest. Enjoy your visit and send my love to Grace."

Ella put on her hat and jacket and started out the door. "I will. Get some rest. I will make a batch of biscuits this evening. Those are always nice to have with an upset stomach."

"Thank you, Ella. That sounds lovely." Mattie crawled back in the bed, pretending to curl up for a long rest.

As soon as she heard the wagon drive away, Mattie began busily packing her things. She left a note of thanks on her bedside table. It felt terrible leaving Ella like this but there was no other choice. The note replaced the spot held by the giraffe. Grabbing her bag, she walked out the door in the direction of town.

The jury selection had produced twelve honest men. Joe was pleased. No one in the jury was tied in any way to the feud. All were hard-working men, a true group of Billy's peers. All except one old codger, Rondal. He was as old as the hills themselves and as unpleasant a man as you will find. Even with his faults though, he was just. That's all that mattered. He along with the eleven others were taking part in the most controversial case of Sheriff Lawson's career. It was important that they were of high character. Joe reviewed the list.

Berl Adams-father of four-farmer
Lee Campbell-father of eight-farmer
Edward Spencer-blacksmith
Thomas Brewer-father of five-farmer
Rondal Gross-farmer
Andy Graham-father of two-farmer
John Sizemore-farmer
Kenneth Arnold-father of three-bank cashier
Eugene Bush-carpenter
Earl Holiday-father of seven-farmer
Bernard Whisman-father of four-sawmill worker
Nicholas Trent-father of two-farmer
Averitt Hollon-father of eight-farmer

Joe placed the list in his desk and began preparation for the trial. There was much to do before next week.

Mattie arrived in her hometown mid-morning. The leaves were beginning to change and the air was getting cooler, hinting of the winter to come. It was a long walk to the home of her parents. Luckily the day was pleasant and a long walk sounded inviting. Mr. Hobbs stepped out from his store to sweep his front stoop. Catching a glimpse of the red-headed, young lady that just arrived, he immediately recognized the familiar smile.

"Mrs. Mattie! I haven't seen you for quite some time. It's good to see you! How have you been?"

Mattie knew she would not be able to answer this honestly. She was relieved that he knew nothing of the trial or the nightmare that had been plaguing her the past year.

"I'm well, Mr. Hobbs. And you?"

"Oh, you know, nothing much changes around here. Is your daddy coming to pick you up? Would you like to have a seat while you wait?"

"Actually, my folks aren't aware I have arrived. I'm getting ready to walk that way."

"No. No. Absolutely not! My nephew is here helping me. I'm getting old, you know?" He chuckled at his admission. "I have a wagon right here. I'll have him give you a ride. I insist."

"Oh, Mr. Hobbs. I don't mind walking. It's a beautiful day. I really don't want you to go to the trouble."

"No trouble at all. What kind of man would I be if I let you take that long trek alone? Why...I wouldn't be able to sleep tonight. You don't want an old man to lose his sleep, now do you, Mrs. Mattie?" He grinned at Mattie and she knew there was no use arguing with him. She graciously accepted his offer.

Mr. Hobbs went inside the store to retrieve his nephew. The two stepped out and Mr. Hobbs introduced them. "Mattie, this is my sister's boy, Ira Akers. He is in from Virginia and has been helping me out and learning how to manage the store. I am hoping he will take over when I'm gone. Ira, this is Mrs. Mattie Akers...no relation to your family. Say, Mrs. Mattie, how is Billy?"

Mattie hoped Mr. Hobbs couldn't see her cheeks flushed. "He is...doing well. He is well, Mr. Hobbs. Thank you for asking."

Mr. Hobbs smiled. "Good, good...Ira, if you could help Mrs. Mattie with her bags and take her to the Abner place for me. I'd appreciate it."

"Yes, sir."

Mattie gave Ira her bag and he assisted her onto the wagon. They rode down the road toward her childhood home.

Ira was quiet and said very little on their trip. Mattie was relieved. Making conversation was exhausting. Sitting quietly and enjoying the ride was a relief.

Ira arrived at the Abner farm and assisted Mattie with her bags. Returning to the store he was dumbstruck. Mattie was the most beautiful woman he had ever seen.

# CHAPTER 13

Matilda approached the front door expecting the comfort of her mama and daddy's company. What she received was a cold welcome. "Hey, Mama, I'm home." The look on her mother's face was stern.

"Well, are you now? We haven't heard from you for months. Lizzie stopped me in town and told me Billy was in jail. Your daddy went to your house only to find it deserted. We had no idea where you were! You could have been dead for all we knew. Then we get a letter from Virginia? Matilda Grace...what is going on?!"

Mattie was ashamed. "I'm sorry Mama. I had hoped you wouldn't find out. Mr. Hobbs didn't know so I thought maybe word hadn't gotten here yet. I should have told you, but everything happened so fast. It's all a blur."

"Word hasn't gotten around yet, but that's only because Lizzie isn't a gossip. Her sister lives in Clay County and wrote her the news."

Mattie's daddy walked through the door. He stopped and looked at Mattie. She could see the hurt in his face. Expecting a lecture from him as well, she apologized upfront. "I'm so sorry Daddy. I didn't mean to worry you."

His face went from disappointment to concern. He walked toward his daughter and embraced her. "Are you ok, darlin'?"

"No sir. Not really." Mattie allowed herself to weep as her daddy held her in his strong arms.

Soon Mama wrapped her arms around them both. They stood like that for a long time until Daddy spoke up. "Here, give me your things and I'll take them to your bed. Sit here and get something to eat. You can tell us what happened."

Mama's face had softened as she prepared a plate of biscuits, green beans, and fatback. They began to eat silently. Daddy soon joined them. No words were said as they ate from their plates. Mattie was unsure of how much she wanted to tell them. Some of it was so difficult to talk about, especially to her father. She knew glossing over some of it will be necessary.

After everyone was finished, Daddy sat back. "Alright, Matilda, let's hear it. Why is Billy in jail?"

Mattie started slowly by telling of how Frank Prewitt came to fix Billy's boots. The uneasiness she felt when she was around him and the hunting trip that Billy took that fateful night. The noise she heard that awoke her in the night. The attack and how hard she fought for her life and the life of their unborn child. She described the blows with the ax, severing Frank's head. She continued until she admitted the latest sin, lying to Billy.
"I just can't tell him there's no baby. I can't."

Her parents sat speechless. She could see the anger in her father's face. She knew he was thinking about all that had happened and his helplessness in doing anything about it. Mama was looking down at the table, tears streaming down her face. Daddy took a long, deep breath.

"Billy knew better than to leave you alone with that man."

"Daddy it's not his fault. Frank chose his actions."

"Billy has some blame in this, too. You can't tell me he doesn't. His boots could have been fixed another day. He knew you were uncomfortable. He knew it! That old Frank Prewitt would come up this way a few times a year. I knew he couldn't be trusted. Any idiot would know that."

"Daddy…"

"I'm glad you killed him."

"I'm going to Clay County to tell them the truth Daddy. I can't let Billy take the blame for this."

"He should take the blame for it. He opened the door for it to happen!"

"My mind is made up."

"No, Matilda. You'll not only be in danger of hanging, you'll be a target for the Caudills. I knew marrying that boy was a mistake. No feud is going to take my daughter. I forbid it."

"Forbid it?? You can't forbid it. I am going to Clay County and you can't stop me."

"I forbid it."

Matilda was stunned.

The first day of the court hearing was proving to be an event. The townspeople filed in, filling the courtroom to capacity. They began lining the walls, choosing to stand. It was becoming obvious that many would have to stand outside and observe. Billy was dumbfounded. He couldn't believe the attention that the trial was receiving. He sat quietly in the courtroom and watched as the people crowded in. He began to wonder what fate had in store for him.

Dan and Charles had ensured that they would get there early and have a seat near the front. It was important that they were able to see who was serving on the jury and study them thoroughly. The jury began filing in. Dan watched carefully. Two immediately stood out. This was proving to be easier than expected.

"All rise, for the honorable Jesse Wilson."

Matilda stared blankly at her father. She could not believe what she was hearing. There was never a time in her life that she could remember feeling angry toward him, but today, she was furious.

"If you will excuse me, Daddy, I'm going to go for a walk."

"I mean what I said, Matilda. I won't allow it."

Mattie ignored his words and walked out the door. She needed to get away and calm down before she said something she would later regret. One thing was for certain, it was time that she took her life back. Walking through the pasture, Mattie spotted her escape. Daddy owned two horses, Red and Tucker. Every night he brought them into the stables. She would get up in the early morning hours and take one of them into town. Mattie was determined to clear Billy's name.

Mattie went to bed early. She said very little throughout the evening. The tension was evident. Going to bed was a relief. She didn't sleep. Instead, she spent the entire night planning her ride to Clay County in the morning. If she left at 3 a.m., she should arrive in Manchester by noon. When she arrived, she would find Sheriff Lawson and tell him everything. She made a promise to Billy but it wasn't supposed to go this far. The weight of this secret, of the trauma she survived, was taking a toll on her. She had to release it.

Mattie could hear her father snoring in the next room. Everyone had been asleep for a few hours. Mattie couldn't wait another minute. Slowly, she slid out of the bed. She followed the same trick that she used as a little girl, making sure to walk along the wall to avoid the creaking boards. When she was little, she used to sneak out the same way to look at the stars. Opening the door just wide enough for her small frame, she slid quietly through. When her feet touched the grass, Mattie released a sigh of relief. She headed in the direction of the stables.

Although she was quite a distance from the house, Mattie was careful to open the barn door quietly. The horses barely stirred as she approached. Reaching to pull the stable door, there appeared to be a problem. Something was hung up. Only a sliver of moonlight was available, but Mattie's eyes were adjusting quickly. Something was hanging on the door. Mattie stopped breathing...it was a padlock! She pulled and yanked at the metal lock purposefully placed between herself and freedom. Checking the other stable, she saw that both had been padlocked by her father. She looked around for something to try and knock it loose. An ax hung on the wall. Memories washed over her. The blood on her nightgown. The pain of Frank Prewitt's brutal attack. The feel of the ax coming down on his throat. Billy sitting behind bars in an effort to protect her. She grabbed it, and using the blunt side, began striking the lock in an effort to break it away.

"Going somewhere?"

Mattie jumped, dropping the ax. She bolted around to see her father standing in the doorway of the barn. For the first time, she felt rage. "How dare you! How DARE YOU!" She ran toward her father, bearing her fists down on his chest. He grabbed her arms to hold her back. As she fought his restraint, she suddenly found herself no longer in her daddy's barn, but in the front room of her and Billy's house. She smelled the mix of tobacco and body odor of Frank Prewitt. She was fighting like a wild animal. Breaking loose from her father's grip, she ran for the door toward the trees.

"Matilda!"

Mattie didn't stop. She ran as fast as she could. She could hear her father calling her name from farther and farther away. She ran until her breath and legs gave way. Hitting the ground, she cried out in wails of rage and torment. She beat her fists on the ground until exhaustion stopped her. The tears flowed freely. She could no longer hear Daddy calling for her.

When Mattie awoke, she was lying on the bed. Her father had searched the woods until he found her unconscious on the cold ground. It was now almost noon. She was trying to remember exactly what happened. The last thing she could recall was discovering the padlock on the stall door. Everything after that was a blur. Daddy must have heard her stirring. He poked his head inside the doorway.

"I see you're awake. How are you feeling?"

"I'm not sure. I'm trying to remember what happened." Mattie lifted her hand to her head and realized both of her lower arms were wrapped in bandages. They were aching. "What happened to my arms?"

Daddy walked in and pulled a chair up beside the bed. "That's a mighty good question. I was going to ask you the same thing. What happened last night?"

"I was going to take one of the horses and ride to Clay County. My plan was to find Sheriff Lawson and tell him my side of the story. Billy didn't kill Frank Prewitt, Daddy. I did. I wanted to tell the sheriff what Frank did to me and why I did it. I couldn't believe you locked the stable doors. I just couldn't believe it. I grabbed the ax and started beating it. That's all I remember. I woke up here and my arms are in bandages and sore. I have no idea why."

Daddy studied her face while she spoke. He rubbed his face with his hands and drew in a deep breath. "What happened isn't important. It's over now. I'm not sure I could explain it anyway. What do you think Sheriff Lawson is going to say when you tell him? Do you actually think he will believe you? Frank is gone. It's just your word. I can't let you hang, Matilda. I can't."

"I can't let Billy hang, Daddy! Let the Caudills come for me. I don't care!"

"I'm sorry. You'll get no help from me." He got up and walked out the door. Mattie heard the front door slam. She felt helpless and alone. Mama walked in.

"Are you hungry? You should eat."

"No, ma'am. No thank you."

Mama sat down in the chair beside the bed. "I know it's difficult for you Matilda. I know what you are saying is true. But I also know that people will talk. They will think you wanted Frank to do those things to you...that if you hadn't, you would have fought harder. I know it's wrong and it doesn't make sense, but it's the truth. And the Caudills, they're a powerful bunch. We can't let you go into the lion's den. You might not come out. The Akers will take care of their own and we'll take care of ours."

Mattie said nothing.

LISA BUSH

# CHAPTER 14

Billy sat in the courtroom stunned by witness accounts. It was obvious that the Caudills were plotting against him. Melissa Elam's testimony had surprised him most. He had always thought highly of her, almost forgetting she was a distant relative of the Caudills. He couldn't understand why she was turning on him. Why were any of them turning on him? He had avoided the feud, done everything and anything to do so. What was the motive? He turned to find his father in the crowd. He was staring at the witness stand with contempt. Bob knew exactly what was happening. The Caudills were using Billy to get back at him. If they succeeded, his son's blood was on his hands.

Dan Caudill sat in the courtroom carefully studying the jury. The rumor in town was that Thomas Brewer had a bad crop this year. He wasn't sure how he was going to feed his family through the winter. Apparently, a blight had spread through his crops and destroyed almost everything. There was little food put up for winter and no money for basic goods. Dan overheard a group of ladies talking about another jury member, Berl Adams, having a sick child at home. His three-year-old son, John, was in poor health and needed to see a doctor in Lexington. The local doctor had tried everything he knew to help him but was at a loss as to how to treat the boy. He suggested seeing a specialist in the bigger city but that costs money; money that Berl doesn't have. They fear that they may lose him. Dan knew one thing for certain; a man desperate to protect his family will forego some of his morals. Dan was counting on that.

Later that afternoon, Dan made his way to the home of Berl and Gale Adams. Gale sat on the porch looking tired. "How do you do, Dan? What brings you out today?"

"Hello there, Gale. I was hoping to talk to Berl. Is he around?"

"He's out in the barn doing some work. This jury duty has him running behind. Isn't that trial something else?"

"Yes ma'am it is. How's the rest of the family?"

"Pretty good, except for John. Doctor isn't sure what's wrong with him. He's mighty sick, won't eat. He's wasting away. There might be some doctors in Lexington that can help him but that takes money, not a lot of that around here."

"My, my, my, that's a shame. I sure hate to hear that. I'm going to get over there and talk to Berl. It was good seeing you, Gale. We'll be praying for little John."

"Thank you, Dan. Good talking to you."

Dan walked toward the barn in search of Berl. He found him inside working. When Dan walked in, Berl looked up from his bench. "Hey there, Dan. What brings you around?"

"Oh not much, just thought I would stop by and say hello. That was some day in court today, huh?"

"Yessir, it was. I'm not allowed to talk about that though, seeing as I am on the jury. But you're right, there sure were a lot of people there today."

"That is the truth, ain't it? I was talking to Gale and she was telling me that your boy hasn't been feeling well. That's a shame."

"He was born sickly. Doctor has tried everything to get him well. Nothing works. The only thing left is to take him to some doctors in Lexington that might have more knowledge about it. We'll have to save up money for that. We're just praying he makes it through the winter."

Dan shook his head in disbelief. "That's awful, Berl. I hate to hear that. I surely do."

Berl went back to his work. "So, Dan, I know you didn't come out here just to talk. What can I do for you? You need something?"

"Well, I really did want to talk about the murder trial. I

wanted to talk to you about..."

"I can't do it, Dan. I'm not going to talk about it."

"But there's some things you should know about Billy..."

"No, Dan."

"That son of yours needs to go to Lexington. I can make that happen for you, Berl. Hear me out."

"Are you trying to bribe me, Dan? Go on home. Leave now and I'll pretend I didn't hear that."

"Alright, Berl, alright. I'll go. Just think about it."

"Bye, Dan. I'll see you around." Berl went back to work. Dan left disappointed. He had hoped for an easy transaction.

Billy sat in his cell pondering the last two days' events. Sheriff Lawson walked in with the evening meal. "Here you are Billy, there's some supper for you."

"Thanks, sheriff, much obliged. Were there any letters today?"

"No, Billy, no mail today."

Billy was concerned. He hadn't heard from Mattie since his last letter. He felt very alone. Bob Akers walked into the jail. "Good evening, sheriff. May I speak to my son, please?"

"I suppose. I just gave him his supper; I'll be here another half hour or so. I'll be right outside."

"Thank you, Joe." Bob waited for him to leave then turned his attention to Billy. "Mattie left Ella's. There was a letter thanking her for her hospitality with no indication of where she was going. I'm guessing she has gone to her family's place."

Billy felt a sense of relief. He was sure that was where she was staying. "That's fine. She'll be safe there." The relief ignited his appetite and he began eating.

"Things didn't look good for you today, Billy. I'm not going to lie to you. I'm worried."

"They were lying, Daddy, plain and simple."

"I know. I suspect the Caudills are behind all of this. I'm afraid they might try to pay off a juror."

"The members of that jury are fine folks. I have faith that they will do the right thing."

"Even good people can be bought, son"

Billy preferred to believe in the goodness of people, but deep down, he knew his father was right. Thinking about that took him down a road he didn't want to go down right now. "Will you come back by tomorrow and pick up a letter I plan to write to Mattie? Mail it to her folks; they will get it to her."

"Sure, son. I'll do that for you." Bob left the jail saying goodbye to Joe as he left. Joe came in and collected Billy's empty plate.

"There's still time to confess, Billy. If you confess now, maybe they won't hang you. There could have been a good reason, I don't know. If you don't tell the jury, you don't leave them many options."

"I'm not admitting to something I didn't do. If there was more to tell I would have told it by now. Those women are lying. The only dealings I ever had with Frank Prewitt is when he fixed my boots. The jury will see the truth. I'm going home after this."

Joe shook his head and headed home for the night. He was troubled by the confidence Billy continued to show. Billy was unmoved by the direness of his situation. Something hadn't felt right about this since day one and now it was eating at Joe. He couldn't shake the feeling that the wrong person was in jail. He wanted to talk to Matilda but she was gone and Joe had no idea where she might be. Why is she hiding? What does she know? These questions haunted Joe throughout the evening and into the early morning hours.

Berl tucked John into his bed. He ran his hand through his son's blond hair. John lay motionless and weak. The feeling of hopelessness was overwhelming. He sat and watched his son, silently sending a prayer to God for his healing. Gale was standing in the doorway.

"We're losing him."

"I know." Berl spent most of the night contemplating his earlier conversation with Dan.

As Dan laid in the silence of the night considering his next approach, Bob lay a few miles away hoping to God that the sins of the father would not mean the death of a son.

# CHAPTER 15

Billy's night was restless. Sheriff Lawson would be taking the stand tomorrow to present the evidence against him. Billy knew that it didn't look good. He couldn't explain away the blood splatter that was found on the wall without incriminating Mattie. He told the sheriff that it was animal blood, but even Billy knew it sounded unbelievable. He decided the less said the better. What disturbed Billy the most was the possibility that he may never be able to hold his child. The idea of leaving Mattie alone hurt more than the idea of dying. The thought of her being another man's wife was almost unbearable. He had to make the jury believe him. Billy watched the stars through his small window until the whispers of sunrise began to light up the sky.

After breakfast, Mama prepared the wagon in order to go to town for supplies. She asked Mattie to accompany her hoping the outing would lift her spirits. She had barely spoken since the night she found the horse stalls padlocked. Mama knew that someday Mattie would understand their actions. When she has children, she will realize the lengths that you will go to protect them.

Mattie rode quietly alongside her mother. Her arms were still bandaged from her ordeal a few nights before. Mama had been insistent that she go into town with her. She had resisted, but now the cool air and the sun shining did seem to lift her melancholy spirit. She felt less like a prisoner as she rode down the dirt road toward town.

When they arrived at Mr. Hobbs's store they hitched the horse and wagon out front. As Mattie walked up the steps to the front door, Ira looked up from his sweeping. The sight of Mattie took his breath.

"Good morning, Ira. Nice to see you again. Mama, this is Ira Akers. He gave me a ride to the house when I first arrived. Ira, this is my mother, Elizabeth Abner."

"Nice to meet you, ma'am. Nice to see you again, Mrs. Mattie." Ira noticed the bandages on Mattie's arms. "Looks like you've hurt yourself. Nothing serious I hope."

"No, nothing serious." Mattie felt awkward. "Just a little accident, they should heal just fine. We better get in here and pick up our supplies. Bye, Ira."

"Bye Mrs. Mattie." Ira felt flushed. He had to remind himself that Matilda Akers was a married woman.

Mr. Hobbs greeted them as they walked in. "Well, hello ladies! How are you two doing today?"

Mama began gathering the items she needed. "Fine, just fine Mr. Hobbs. I see you've hired some new help."

"Oh, that's my nephew, Ira. He's my sister's boy from up in Virginia. I never had any children and I want to pass this store along to someone when I'm gone. He's learning a little bit about things. He'll be heading back to Virginia for the winter next week. Be moving down here to stay in the spring. It'll be nice to have the help and to be able to slow down a bit."

"Yes, sir. I imagine so." Mama went back to the task of picking up supplies as Mattie followed along behind her.

Suddenly, Mr. Hobbs remembered, "Oh, Mrs. Mattie! I almost forgot a letter came for you today from Billy. You must be planning to stay awhile, I guess." He went behind the counter and retrieved the letter for her. Mattie felt the look of disapproval on Mama's face. She took the letter and held on to it.

"Thank you, Mr. Hobbs." Mama's glare could not extinguish the joy Mattie was feeling. Billy knew where to find her.
*October 20, 1849*

*My Dearest Matilda,*

*You are on my mind day and night. Our family is a guiding light that will lead me out of this jail cell and back into your arms. I pray every night that you are safe and well and that we will be reunited again. Daddy told me you left Ella's. I am hoping that this letter finds you at your mama and daddy's home, safe and sound.*
*This feud is working to destroy me. There are those who are lying. They are claiming they saw things that would incriminate me. I must confess, my love, that I face an uphill climb to my freedom. Remember our promise. Stay where you are and do not come to Clay County. I need you and the baby to stay safe. That is the most important thing. We will get through this and I will hold you again.*

*With all of my love,*

*Billy*

    Matilda was disturbed by the possibility of Billy being sentenced for the murder of Prewitt. She felt both responsible and helpless for the situation that Billy was in. If she had told Sheriff Lawson what had happened at the beginning, maybe it wouldn't have come to this. Why must it be so difficult for a woman to receive justice for being defiled by a man? Why is she seen to be at fault? Billy's concern for her reputation had been part of the guiding force to the promise that she made to him. He wanted to protect her but now he may pay the ultimate price. She wanted to defy his wishes and tell her story. The story of what that treacherous bastard did to her and their baby. Instead, she found herself being held prisoner out of love and protection, her own form of jail. She laid her hand on her empty womb and tried to think of a way to escape.

    "The prosecution would like to call to the stand Sheriff Joseph Lawson."

    Joe approached the bench, placed his hand on the Bible, and swore his oath. After taking a seat, Claude Graham stood to begin his questioning. Graham was an older gentleman and considered quite pompous. He considered himself to be quite the aristocrat even though he owned only one suit that he wore repeatedly on court days with his hair slicked back with Macassar Oil. He confronted Sheriff Lawson confidently.

"Sheriff Lawson, could you please tell us about the discovery found at the farm of the defendant, William Akers?"

"Yes. In the winter of this year, early February actually, Curtis Shearer came to see me in regards to a discovery that his wife Doris had made. Their dog had managed to dig up a head and bring it to their house giving Doris an awful fright. Upon investigation, I concluded that the head belonged to Frank Prewitt, the local shoe cobbler. The Akers farm lies just past the Shearers' place, so I decided to look in the woods and see if I could find where the body might be. After investigating, I discovered a shallow grave in a grove of trees. There I found Frank Prewitt's body. He had been buried with his head placed at his feet."

There was stirring and whispering all throughout the courtroom as the spectators reacted to the shock of the story.

Judge Wilson began pounding his gavel. "Order! Order in the court! I want order I say." A hush fell over the crowd.

Claude shook his head. "That's just awful. Tell me, sheriff, what did you find when you began investigating the home of William Akers?"

"While looking around the farm, I noticed a stain on their ox that I first thought was mud. I found that odd since we hadn't had any rain for quite some time at that point. Upon further investigation, I saw that the stain flaked off. Blood does that. I went into the house and found what appeared to be a bloodstain behind a chair. I can't confirm whether that was the case or not because when I came back, the stain was gone. On that same visit, I noticed what appeared to be blood splatter on the upper part of the wall in the front room of their house. This wall was directly in front of where they store their ax. I also found a potato sack stored in the house which was the same type of sack found with the body of Frank Prewitt."

The courtroom began to stir and a low roar of whispers erupted. The judge again banged his gavel. "Order! Order in this court!"

Claude Graham continued. "Sheriff, you keep referring to *their* ox and *their* ax. Who is the *their* you are speaking of?"

"William Akers and his wife, Matilda Akers."

"I see, I see. And where is Mrs. Matilda Akers today?"

"We don't know actually. Billy won't tell me. She left without a trace. I'm guessing she is with her family in Owsley County, but I don't know."

"No further questions. Thank you, Sheriff Lawson. Your witness."

Everett Thompson stood up to question the lawman. Everett was a stark contrast to Claude with his easy way of moving and speaking. Most folks considered him the smartest man in town. He would disagree, considering himself more of a farmer than a lawyer. His talent at understanding the law made him quite an adversary in the courtroom.

"Good mornin', sheriff. So let me ask you this, how do you know the bloodstains you found was the blood of Frank Prewitt?"

"I don't know. The circumstances surrounding…"

"Just answer the question please, Sheriff Lawson."

Joe shifted in his seat. He was always uncomfortable at cross-examinations. He did not like being cut off. Billy held his head a little higher. He was grateful that his father had retained Everett as his attorney.

"Sheriff Lawson, do the Akers raise any animals?"

"Yes, but this was…"

"Just yes or no if you don't mind, sir. Isn't it possible that the blood you found could be animal blood?"

"It's doubtful since…"

"Yes or no please, Sheriff Lawson."

"I mean, yes, I guess it could be…"

"Thank you, sheriff. Sheriff, I'm curious to know if there were any other injuries that were found on the body of Frank Prewitt."

Billy did not like this line of questioning. This was treading dangerously close to revealing what happened to Mattie on that fateful night. He found his daddy in the crowd of spectators. Bob Akers was stone-faced, waiting for Joe to answer.

"Yes. There were claw marks on the face and what appears to be a deep bite mark on the right hand of the victim."

Everett appeared to be contemplating this revelation. "Claw marks on the cheeks? And a bite mark on his hand? You don't say? Fascinating. If it would please the court, I would like to show the hands of William Akers."

The judge seemed curious himself. "I'll allow it."

"Billy, would you please hold your hands up with your palms facing you and the back of your hands facing the jury?"

Billy did as he was told. Everett turned to face the jury. "Can y'all see that?" Many of the jury members were shaking their heads no.

"Billy, if you could step up here to the jury box please and let these fine people see your fingernails." Billy stepped up to the jury so that they could see his fingernails. "Now Billy, if you would please show the judge and the sheriff." Billy did so. Sheriff Lawson shifted in his seat yet again.

"As you can see, William Akers has very short fingernails, almost no nails at all. Billy have you had them trimmed recently?"

"No, sir."

"Sheriff has Mr. Akers had his nails trimmed while he has been under your supervision?"

"No, he has not."

"That's right because William Akers has a bad habit of biting his nails. Yet, Frank Prewitt had claw marks on his face? Interesting. That is interesting. Makes you wonder where he got those, doesn't it? No further questions."

Judge Wilson appeared concerned. "You may step down. We are going to take a brief recess. We will meet again at 2:00 p.m. Court is adjourned." The gavel hit and the crowd began to disperse. Sheriff Lawson escorted Billy to the jail.

"Let's have some lunch, Billy. We need to talk."

# CHAPTER 16

Joe had convinced himself that the claw and bite marks were from an animal that had gotten to Frank after his death. He had even considered the Shearers' dog, Jack. But now it posed the question of whether or not the claw marks and the bite on the hand could have been made by the killer. If that were true, Billy could not have been the one who killed Frank Prewitt. Joe was in a moral dilemma. He did not want to live with the death of an innocent man on his conscience.

Joe led Billy into his cell and shut the door. Joe's wife had prepared a lunch of soup beans, cornbread, and collard greens. Joe fixed Billy's plate and handed it to him. Pulling up a chair, he talked to Billy as he ate. "Your lawyer, he really threw some doubt at the jury. That was a good move if I do say so myself." He ate a large spoonful of beans and followed it with the warm cornbread.

"Yes, sir. It was." Billy didn't want to say too much.

"Really got me thinking, too. Where do you think those claw marks came from, Billy?"

"I don't know, sheriff, an animal I guess." Billy kept eating, avoiding eye contact.

"I suppose. Yes, I guess that's possible. But, let's just say, for the sake of argument, that they came from the killer. That would mean you could be proven innocent. You could go home, Billy."

"I am innocent, sheriff."

"Well, you keep saying that. You keep saying that you didn't kill Frank but you don't tell me anything, absolutely nothing. There are no witnesses to the murder, only witnesses who saw Frank heading to your place to do some work for you. All of the evidence points to you, Billy. If you won't save yourself, I can't save you, man! Tell me what happened!"

"I don't know what happened."

"I don't believe you." Sheriff Lawson was visibly frustrated. He leaned back in his chair and began to think. He decided to speak aloud one of his earlier suspicions.

"Blood splatter in your house. Blood on your ox. New boards found on the floor near the blood. You admit to burying the body. This is what I think could have happened. Frank did something to your wife, something awful."

Billy stopped eating and looked at the sheriff. Joe noticed the reaction.

"I think he may have done or at least tried to do the most horrible thing a man can do to a woman. Matilda is a strong young woman. She fought him. She may have clawed his face and bit his hand, maybe while he was trying to muffle her screams. Somehow she was able to kill him with the ax. I think you are protecting your wife."

"No. Mattie had nothing to do with this. I found Frank dead in the woods. I told you that."

"Or maybe you walked in on Frank hurting your wife and, in a fit of rage, you killed him."

"I have nothing to say to you sheriff. I'm done with my lunch. Take it." Billy handed his plate through the bars to Joe. His face was cold and stern.

"Dammit, Billy! I can't help you if you don't let me! What the hell happened over there, son?!"

"Nothing. Nothing happened. And I'm not your son. Now leave me be."

Joe was shaken. This turn of events left him with the fear that an innocent man might possibly hang for a murder he didn't commit. He had to find Matilda Akers. He needed to know the truth.

Berl was standing outside rolling a cigarette as he watched the people milling about. Dan approached him.

"Hey, Berl. Sorry about the other day, I guess I was just…"

"It's alright. No harm done."

"Yeah, I guess not. Well, sorry just the same. How's your boy?"

"Not good."

"That's a shame. I hate to hear that. When are you taking him to Lexington?"

"When we save enough money for the trip." He took a long draw from his cigarette. "Not sure when that will be."

"I see." Dan knew that desperation was setting in. He had to be patient.

"Say, Dan, why don't you come by the house tonight. I want to show you some things I've been working on."

"Sure, sure, I can stop by Berl. I'll, um, see you this evening."

Berl kept looking straight ahead, lost in thought. "See you this evening."

Dan walked away before anyone could begin to question why a Caudill was talking to one of the jurors. However, the exchange had already been witnessed from a grove of trees a few yards away where Bob Akers had been watching.

Dan caught up with Charles. "I'm going to Berl's house tonight. I think he is ready to talk business. I need you to go talk to Tom and see how things are with him. As I hear it, he is struggling to feed his family. We need to act fast."

"I'll go by his place after court is over. It should be starting back here directly."

Joe left Billy in his cell and went looking for Judge Wilson. He found him as he was about to enter the courtroom.

"Can I speak to you, judge?"

"Well, this is a bit unorthodox. What is it concerning?"

"I need to request a recess until tomorrow, or maybe a few days. The point Everett Thompson brought up about the fingernails…I need to talk to Billy's wife, Matilda Akers."

"Is that so? You think you might have the wrong man, Joe?"

"I didn't say that. The evidence says that I have the right person in custody. But I want to make sure I have answered any questions I might have."

"Where is his wife?"

"I'm not sure and Billy ain't talking. If I were to guess, I would say she is with her family. I think she is from Owsley County. I was wanting to ride up there and ask around. See if I can find her."

Judge Wilson thought for a moment. "I'll discuss a break with the attorneys. I'll tell them you needed to follow up on something out of town. You need to work fast though. The best I can do is to give you 'til Monday. That's four days. If you don't have anything by then, we have to move on."

"Yes, sir. Thank you, Your Honor."

Joe went home and arranged for Billy's meals while he was away for the next couple of days. He called on his friend, Luther to take care of the jail while he was gone. With everything in place, Joe went to bed early preparing for his trip the next morning.

Dan stepped inside the barn where Berl was sharpening some of his farm tools. "Hey there, Berl. What is it you wanted to show me?"

Berl stopped what he was doing and turned around to face him. Dan noticed he looked tired. "You ok, Berl?"

"He's dying, Dan. My boy is dying and the only thing that might save him is if we can get him to Lexington. I need to know...is that offer still on the table?"

"Yes. That it is, Berl."

"What do you want me to do?"

Dan reached in his pocket and gave Berl the $20 he had brought. Berl looked at the money and then looked at Dan waiting for the answer.

I need you to make sure Billy Akers hangs."

# CHAPTER 17

Joe was on his horse, Bullet, at daybreak riding in the direction of Owsley County. He wanted to be there by early afternoon. As the cold morning turned to midday, he arrived in town. He hitched his horse and went into the general store. Storekeepers knew everyone, so this was his best chance of finding Matilda, or at least her family members. Mr. Hobbs was behind the counter adding up Imogene Spencer's order.

"Good morning there, young man. Can I help you?"

Joe smiled at the friendly gentleman. "Yes, sir. But I'm not in a hurry. It can wait until you're finished."

"Oh ok. Shouldn't be long."

Joe wandered about the store. Imogene was very interested in this stranger. "I don't think I've seen you around here before. Where are you from?"

"Clay County, ma'am. I'm the sheriff there. The name is Joe, Joe Lawson. A pleasure to meet you." He tipped his hat at Imogene.

Mr. Hobbs stopped what he was doing and looked at the sheriff. "The sheriff! Oh my, is there any trouble?" He and Imogene looked at each other surprised and intrigued.

"Oh no, nothing to be concerned about. I'm just needing to get in contact with someone that may live here. Are either of you familiar with Matilda Akers?"

"Mrs. Mattie!" Mr. Hobbs was shocked to hear that she was

the one the sheriff was looking for. "She is staying with her folks. They live up that road heading east. Just follow it and it will take you directly to her farm. Nothing is wrong with Billy is there?"

Joe realized that news of the trial hadn't made it here yet. "No, no, nothing like that. I just have a few questions. Thank you for the information. You folks have a nice day." He tipped his hat at them both and headed out the door.

As Imogene was loading her wagon, George Abner walked by. "Here Imogene, let me give you a hand."

"Oh thank you, George. I do appreciate it. Hey, the sheriff of Clay County just stopped by the store a few minutes ago. He's headed to your place to talk to Mattie. I hope everything is ok."

"My place? Talk to Mattie? Which way was he headed?"

"Mr. Hobbs sent him down the main road. You ok?"

"Oh yes, I'm fine Imogene. Thanks for letting me know. Looks like you are loaded and ready. We'll see you around." It was an effort to act calm when he wanted to race back home.

"Thank you, George. Tell Elizabeth hello."

"Will do. Bye, now."

George Abner walked calmly to his horse and mounted it, trying to remain calm. He had to move fast. The sheriff could not get to Mattie. He would have to cut him off on the way. George knew he would have to run Tucker hard through a clearing on the other side of the wood line to get ahead of the sheriff. When he and Tucker got to the pasture, he kicked hard, "Hyah!" Tucker obediently went into a gallop, George was running him as fast as he could push him. He was hoping that the sheriff was going at a steady pace and hadn't gotten much of a head start. He ran Tucker to the area where he thought he might be able to cut off the lawman and slowed down. He and his horse began winding through the woods until they reached the main road. It was empty. They were either too early or too late. George waited nervously.

Within a few minutes, George recognized hoof beats coming down the road. He clucked for Tucker to trot in the direction of the oncoming traveler. As they moved forward, a figure on his horse came into view.

"Hello there! Can I help you?"

Joe was startled to come upon anyone but guessed that this could be a member of the Abner family. "Hello! Yes, I was looking for the Abner place."

"I'm George Abner. What can I do for you?"

"I'm Sheriff Joe Lawson from Clay County. I was needing to speak to Matilda Akers. Is she your daughter by chance?"

"She is. But she's not home. She and her mother are visiting family. What is this concerning?"

He hoped that the sheriff would believe the lie and turn around.

"I was needing to ask her some questions about Billy. I'm surprised that she hasn't been by to see him. She left the farm suddenly and hasn't been back. Mighty odd. I would like to find out why."

"Well, I can go ahead and tell you. She isn't a part of anything that Billy Akers or that feud has going on. She is where she needs to be."

Joe was now picking up on the fact that Mr. Abner was protecting his daughter. "I see. Well, I'm sure you understand that I would like to hear that from her. This is a very important case. Her husband could hang."

"Would serve him right." George blurted out. "The Akers are nothing but trouble. She should have never married him. You can be moving along, sheriff. This isn't your town. We have no business here to discuss."

Joe sat on his horse looking in the eyes of Matilda's father. "With all due respect Mr. Abner, I beg to differ. If you change your mind, I'll be staying in town for a night or two. I would appreciate it if you let Mattie know I am looking for her." With that, he clucked to his horse Bullet and rode back in the direction of town.

Charles approached the home of Thomas Brewer with a basket full of fruits and vegetables that Esther had prepared for the winter. There were enough beans, turnips, peppers, and some jelly to last a family the size of the Brewers a couple of weeks, as long as they rationed it properly. Charles set the basket down on the porch and knocked on the door. Thomas's wife, Edna, answered.

"Charles! Hello! What brings you here?"

Charles picked up the basket and presented it to Edna. She looked as though she had just seen a mirage. "Esther wanted to send you a few things from our garden. We heard about the blight that y'all had and we wanted to share some of our harvest with you, seeing as we had a good crop this year."

Edna took the basket from him. "Oh my! Thank you, Charles. Thank you so much! Be sure to tell Esther thank you also. You just don't know..." Edna was beginning to tear up.

"Now, now, Edna, don't cry. We were glad to do it. Neighbors helping neighbors, that's what the Good Book teaches us."

"Well, don't just stand there. C'mon in. I'll go get Thomas and let him know you are here. He will be glad to see you!"

Charles stepped into the small cabin. He could hear Edna yelling for Thomas out the back door. She came back to the front room.

"Thomas is out back dressing a deer. He said if you like you can come back there. He's pretty proud of his kill today!" Edna was obviously proud too.

"Yes ma'am. I need to go see for myself. Thank you, Edna."

Charles went to the back of the cabin and stepped out. Thomas was field dressing a large buck. Charles let out a whistle. "That is a nice looking buck you got there, Tom. Looks like you've had a good day."

"I found this one just over the hill here. I hadn't been gone an hour or so. The good Lord knew we needed it, I reckon." He couldn't stop smiling. This deer meat was going to help ensure his family didn't starve to death this winter.

"That deer will taste mighty good with the basket that Esther sent. We brought some things from the garden that she had already preserved for winter. I heard about that blight y'all had. What a shame."

"Thank you, Charles. That sure is neighborly of you. Much appreciated too, I can tell you that. The Lord is good."

"Yes, he is. What about court being delayed till Monday? That's something, ain't it?"

"Yeah, I don't know what all that is about. I wish I had never been called on that jury. I got too much going on here to deal with all that."

"Yes, sir. You definitely have your hands full here. How many kids you got?"

"Seven. And Edna thinks she may be expectin' another one. I'm gonna have to build a bigger house!"

Charles chuckled. "Yes, I believe you are! So, what do you think about the case so far? You think Billy did it?"

Thomas stopped cleaning the deer for a minute. "I'm not supposed to talk about it. All I know is that I don't know. This is an odd case and I wish I didn't have anything to do with it."

"Did you know Frank Prewitt was one of our kinfolk?"

"No, I didn't. Is that right? Nothing against you, but I wasn't real fond of Frank. He was good at repairing shoes, but he was a strange feller. He made Edna uncomfortable. I never left her alone with him."

"You know his own sister didn't even like him."

"Is that right? That says something right there."

"It does. It does. Still, murder is wrong. We can't be killing everyone we don't like."

"No. Interesting thing to say, coming from a Caudill." Thomas looked at Charles and gave a little wink.

Charles laughed nervously. "I guess you're right, Tom. I can't argue with you there."

Thomas chuckled and went back to his deer.

"You know, Tom…this deer is going to help your situation a good while. But you're going to need more if your family is going to make it through the winter. I can help you out, you know."

Thomas stopped and looked at Charles. He studied his face as though he hoped to read his mind. "How?"

"Well, we had a good crop this year and there is plenty to share. I could also give you some money to help you with dry goods for the winter from Hobbs's Store."

"I don't take charity, Charles. You know me better than that."

"Oh, I know that, Tom. Believe me, I know that. This wouldn't be charity. I'd be paying you for something really important, a little job you could say."

"What kind of job?"

Charles pulled the money out of his pocket. "This is $15 here. It's yours if you can get me a guilty verdict for Billy Akers."

Thomas looked at the money. It would go a long way to feeding his family. "I don't know Charles. That feels wrong."

"Listen, Tom, we know that Frank was probably killed by Bob. He either killed him or had a hand in it. Billy chose his place in this feud. That's on him. Remember Elijah? There has been no justice for him. None! It's not right Tom! You know it and I know it. You need food and we need justice. What do you say, Tom?"

Thomas was looking at the ground. This was a struggle of the soul. The door slammed and his daughter Emily ran out to him.

"Papa! We have jelly in the house! Mr. Caudill brought it for us...thank you, Mr. Caudill!" She hugged Charles's leg and ran back toward the house. "Mama said she may have enough flour for biscuits!" She swung open the door and ran back inside.

Thomas stared at the back door, lost in thought. He turned back to Charles. "I'll do it."

Charles handed him the money. "Thank you, Tom. You're doing the right thing."

Thomas took the money. Right or wrong, he had to feed his family.

# CHAPTER 18

Matilda was feeding the chickens when her daddy rode in. The injuries on her arms were barely visible. She had been watching her father closely, trying to figure out where he hid the keys to the padlocks in the barn. This was a waiting game. Once she knew where he kept them, she would have to be vigilant to catch him when his guard was down. That was the only way she could escape and save Billy from conviction.

George dismounted and led Tucker to the barn. Locking him in the stall he glanced at Mattie and, without a word, went into the house. Something had happened. Something strange was going on. Mattie threw the last of the chicken feed on the ground and made her way to the window. She could hear Daddy talking to Mama in the kitchen.

"I don't want you taking Mattie to town tomorrow. The Clay County sheriff is here and he's looking for her. I got rid of him today, but he's determined. I don't want her knowing anything about it. I'll tell her I need her to do something around here."

Mattie couldn't believe it. Joe was here and he was just a stone's throw away. She wouldn't have to worry about the keys, Joe could take her back to Billy. She had to act fast. All she knew to do was run. She began running down the road toward town.

"Mattie!"

Mattie could hear her daddy yelling through the kitchen window. She knew he would be right behind her shortly. She had to run as fast and as hard as she could if she was going to make it to Sheriff Lawson. She heard the door slam and the sound of footsteps. She dare not turn around. Her focus had to be on the destination.

"Mattie!"

She could feel the tears wanting to fall. This was no time for that. All of her energy had to be focused on her legs and the road ahead. She ran harder. She was a quarter of the way there.

"I'm coming, Billy," she whispered to the wind.

The footsteps were getting closer. She could hear the labored breath of her father behind her. He was getting closer. Please, God, let someone come down the road and see her. She felt him run past her. He turned around and blocked her from going further.

"Matilda! Stop!"

"I'm going, Daddy! You can't stop me. I'm going to see the sheriff!"

She tried going around him but he grabbed her arms and held her. She tried pulling away.

"Stop it, Mattie."

"Let me go!"

George pushed his daughter to the ground. "I said stop it. You're not going."

Mattie felt the rage well up inside of her. She picked herself up and charged at her father. She felt the slap of the back of his hand against the side of her face. The sting was numbing. It knocked her back to the ground. Mattie was stunned. The only other man that had hit her like that was Frank Prewitt. She sat staring back at her father, dumbfounded.

"I said you aren't going. Get back to the house. Now."

Mattie picked herself up. She didn't cry. She didn't scream. She felt nothing.

"I hate you." She turned and walked back to the house. Her father watched her as she walked proudly back to her personal prison. Everything had changed.

Mattie walked into the house and went straight to her room. Mama followed behind and stood in the doorway. "Are you alright?" Mattie lay silent, staring at the ceiling. Her face reddened by the blow from her father.

Mama heard George walk in. "What happened?"

"I saved her."

Joe decided to get a room for the night at the boarding house in town. Thelma Pritchard had been running her establishment for the past thirty years. Her hospitality, along with her attention to detail, had made her clients the most comfortable in eastern Kentucky. She welcomed the sheriff, getting him checked in. "Looks like you might be a sheriff or deputy of some sort. Where are you from?"

"Yes, ma'am. I'm the sheriff of Clay County, just here for a little business."

"Oh, I see. Nothing bad I hope." She chuckled, completely unaware of what was at stake. "Here is your key. Your room is upstairs, first door on the left. I have you in room number 3. I fix breakfast every morning at 8 a.m. if you would like to join us."

"Thank you, ma'am. I believe I will. That sounds delicious. Appreciate it."

He went upstairs and got settled in. He had hoped talking to Matilda would be less complicated. Word must have gotten to her father that he was in town. It was as if he had been expecting him. Joe was going to have to figure out another way of getting the answers he needed. The storekeeper seemed to know Billy. That would probably be a good start.

After settling in, Joe walked into Mr. Hobbs's general store. "Well, hello again, sheriff! Back again I see. Were you able to find Mrs. Mattie?"

"No, she is out of town with her mother visiting family. I wasn't able to talk to her."

Mr. Hobbs appeared confused. "I didn't know they went out of town. I thought Mrs. Abner was coming by tomorrow to pick up the fabric I ordered for her. Oh well, guess I'll hold it 'til they get back."

"Something must have come up. Family matter I guess." Joe thought it might be a good idea to stick close to town tomorrow. He might get lucky and run into Mrs. Abner. "So I stopped by to pick up some tobacco if you don't mind."

"Absolutely! Word to the wise, don't smoke in Thelma's boarding house. She'll run you out of there." Mr. Hobbs winked and smiled, handing a pouch of tobacco to Joe.

Joe laughed. "Thanks for the warning." He paid for the tobacco and thanked him. He would be keeping a close eye on the store tomorrow.

Mrs. Abner got the wagon ready to go to town early. She was so angry with her husband after learning of his striking Matilda the day before. They had wanted to protect their daughter, but now it felt corrupt. She had not slept the night before thinking about the situation. Mattie had done nothing wrong, she had been the victim of a vicious attack and saved herself. Her husband sat in a jail cell, a victim of his name and his great love for his wife. This was all wrong. George had wanted her to stay home until he was sure that the sheriff was out of town. Elizabeth had told him that she had never met the man and he would have no idea who she was. She also informed him that he was becoming more of a warden than a family man. With the wagon ready, she got on and clucked to the horses.

Joe was up early. He had been watching the store carefully for any customers who looked like they might be from the Abner place. He was lucky that his window at the boarding house gave him a perfect view. Things had remained fairly quiet, but it was early. He could smell bacon frying downstairs so he stepped away from his post to enjoy some of Thelma's breakfast.

"That was delicious, ma'am. I won't be able to eat the rest of the day!"

"Oh now, I doubt that very seriously. I haven't met a man yet who would pass on a meal."

Joe smiled and stepped outside for a smoke. He heard an approaching wagon and noticed one was coming from the road that led to the Abners. He backed away, hoping to not be noticed. He could only assume that it might be Mrs. Abner.

As the wagon stopped in front of the store, Joe could see now that it was a woman driving. This may be the break he was looking for. He watched quietly out of sight as she went into the store and then made his way closer to wait. He could hear the friendly voice of the storekeeper.

"Well hello there, Mrs. Abner! I didn't expect to see you here today. I heard you were out of town visiting family. I have your fabric right here."

"Thank you, Mr. Hobbs. Yes, I'm back." She hated lying but her husband had left her no choice. "Thank you for getting this fabric for me. It will work just perfectly."

"Glad to do it, ma'am. By the way, the sheriff from Clay County is staying over at Miss Thelma's boarding house. He's been looking for Mrs. Matilda. Should I send him your way if I see him?"

"No that won't be necessary. It's all been taken care of. Thanks again, Mr. Hobbs. See you next week."

Joe was waiting in the grass just behind the front of the store. As Mrs. Abner walked toward her wagon, Sheriff Lawson followed behind her.

"Let me help you with that, Mrs. Abner."

"Oh thank you, that won't be necessar..." Elizabeth stopped abruptly as she turned and realized that the man offering assistance was not a familiar face. No doubt it was the sheriff.

I'm sorry, I don't believe I know you, sir."

"I do apologize ma'am. I am Sheriff Joe Lawson from Clay County. I am trying to locate Matilda Abner. Aren't you her mother?"

"I am. I'm afraid Matilda is out of town visiting family. Would you like for me to give her a message?"

"Oh, I see. That's funny because your husband told me you both were. It wouldn't be that you are keeping Matilda hidden from me, are you?"

"Well, I'm not sure what business that would be of yours. If you have a message for her I can pass it along. Otherwise, I will be on my way."

Joe knew Matilda was being hidden by her family and getting to her was seeming less and less likely. "I appreciate that,

Mrs. Abner. If you could please tell your daughter that if she knows anything important about the death of Frank Prewitt, if there is anything that she knows that I don't, now is the time to tell me. Billy is about to hang. I understand you want to protect Matilda, but I'm sure you do not want the blood of your son-in-law on your hands."

Elizabeth straightened her back and looked directly at Sheriff Lawson. "Do you have any children, sheriff?"

"No, ma'am. The good Lord never blessed us with any."

"Then you absolutely do NOT understand. I suggest you do your job and stop putting the guilt on other people for your poor investigation." And with that, Elizabeth climbed into the wagon and clucked to her horse. Joe stood stunned.

As Elizabeth rode down the road, she refused to look back. She could not allow the sheriff to think that she regretted their exchange. She could also not allow him to see the tears streaming down her face.

As she walked through the front door, George Abner was standing in the kitchen. "Did you have any trouble?"

Elizabeth turned to him with a cold glare. "I have nothing to say to you. Our daughter's broken heart and the blood of Billy Akers are on your conscience. Now leave me be."

George Abner said nothing.

# CHAPTER 19

Joe rode home with the impending court proceedings weighing heavily on his mind. His trip to Owsley County had turned up empty. He knew that if he could have spoken to Mattie, he may have found the answers he needed. Before going home, he stopped by to see Marcus and discuss the injuries to Frank's face and hand.

"Hey, Marcus, are you here?" Joe shouted out as he walked through the front door.

"I'll be right there. Just finishing up some paperwork." Marcus stepped into the front office. "Hello, Joe. What can I do for you?"

"I have some questions for you about Frank Prewitt. When we found him there were some claw marks on his face and what looked like a bite in the palm of his hand. Do you think those were made by an animal?"

Marcus thought for a minute and shook his head. "It's hard to say, very well could have been. If it were an animal, I find it strange that it didn't make a meal out of him, especially in the dead of winter."

"You have a point, Marcus. I just don't know…"

"Are you questioning whether Billy Akers did it or not, sheriff?" Marcus looked concerned. He knew that if convicted, Billy could hang for the crime.

"I'm not sure. The claw marks are haunting me. If Billy were fighting Frank he could have easily overpowered him. There was no need to claw at him. There was no way Frank could have gotten the upper hand on Billy, not for long at least. I'm missing something and I can't get to the ones who have the answers."

"Where's Matilda?"

"She's staying with family in Owsley County. They won't let me near her. To be honest, I'm beginning to wonder if she is there by choice."

"You have a lot on your plate, Joe. I don't envy you, not one bit."

"Unfortunately, you're right. Thank you, Marcus. I better get home and see the wife. Take care."

"See you around, Joe."

Joe was about to mount his horse and ride home when he heard footsteps approaching. He turned to find Bob Akers approaching fast.

"I need to talk to you, sheriff. I've been looking for you for two days."

"I've been out of town on business. What seems to be the problem?"

"I'll tell you what the problem is. The Caudills are paying off jurors. I know they are! I saw Dan talking to Berl the other day. Something's up and you need to fix it!"

"Whoa there, Bob. Slow down. Those are strong accusations you're making. Berl is a good man, it's hard for me to believe he could be bought."

"Berl is a good man, sheriff. But he has a sick boy who, from what I hear, isn't far from death. That makes him a desperate man. The Caudills wouldn't care at all to take advantage of that, especially if it meant getting back at me."

As difficult as it was for Joe to believe that any of the jurors could be bought, Bob had made a valid point. A desperate man would push his morals aside to save his family. This new dilemma complicated things even more. Bob was obviously upset, but the fact remained, there was no proof except for a conversation witnessed by the father of the defendant.

"Bob, you can't be thinking that every conversation held

by a Caudill is a plot against you. But I can see that you're upset, so I'll look into it. I've got to get home, but tomorrow I'll stop by Berl's and talk to him."

"Alright, sheriff. But mark my word, it's happening." Bob turned and stomped off. Joe watched him walk away and then mounted his horse to head home. He needed some rest. As he rode through town, he passed Thomas Brewer loading his wagon.

"Hello, Tom. Need any help?"

"No, thank you, sheriff. I think I got it."

"Looks like you're getting ready for winter. Now that's a load of supplies! Think that's enough for all those youngins of yours?" Joe smiled, but Thomas felt the guilt building.

"I hope so, sheriff. I hope so. Guess I'll see you on Monday. Bye, now." Thomas climbed on his wagon and headed home.

Joe rode along toward home when a realization hit him. Thomas had a wagon full of goods for the winter. Right now he was probably the poorest man in Clay County. Where did he get the money for that? Bob's words were becoming more difficult to ignore.

Thomas arrived home and began unloading his day's purchases. Edna's eyes grew wide as she saw all of the food he had purchased. "Thomas! How on earth did you get all of this?"

Thomas smiled at his wife. "I did some work for Dan Caudill and he paid me well. This should get us through winter, Edna. We're going to make it." He kissed his wife on the cheek as she stared in disbelief.

The children came in to see what their daddy had brought. "Daddy! There's so much food!" The oldest daughter, Cora Lee, was in awe. Emily was over the moon.

"Daddy, did you bring sweet cakes?" She smiled hopefully.

Cora Lee scolded her, "Emily! Don't be selfish."

"I did bring sweet cakes, baby girl!" Thomas picked his daughter up swinging her around as she squealed. "We deserve a little treat I do believe."

Edna was worried. Thomas had not been gone long

enough to have done a job that brought this much money. The Caudills did well but even they wouldn't be able to shop like this for their families. Thomas noticed the look of worry on his wife's face. Something didn't seem right.

"Everything alright, darlin'? I thought you'd be happy."

Edna smiled. "I am, Thomas, I am. I'm just surprised I think. This is wonderful. Thank you. You have always taken good care of us. The good Lord blessed me when I found you." Thomas, for the first time in a long while, welled up with pride.

After church services, Joe decided he would ride out to Berl's and have a talk with him. Seeing Thomas the day before with what appeared to be a sudden windfall, had Joe worried that Bob Akers's accusations were true. Joe took his wife home and promised he would be back in time for Sunday dinner.

Joe arrived at Berl's place and knocked on the door of the small cabin. Gale greeted him. "Well hello there, sheriff. What brings you here? You're just in time for dinner. C'mon in."

"Thank you, Gale, but I won't be staying for dinner. I promised my wife I would be back in time to eat with her at home. I won't be but a minute. Is Berl around?"

"Yes, he's in the barn. Everything alright?"

"Yes ma'am. I just need to ask him a question. Thank you again for the dinner invitation. It sure smells awfully good."

Gale smiled and went back to preparing the meal. "Well, if you change your mind there is plenty."

Joe walked to the barn and found Berl working. "It's Sunday, Berl, you're supposed to be resting."

Berl looked up surprised. "Hello there, Joe. I could say the same for you. What brings you out?" Berl was feeling a bit squeamish.

"Oh, nothing in particular. I just got back to town, had a little business elsewhere. I heard you request prayer for your boy this morning. Is he still not well?"

"He's in bad shape. Wasting away. We're taking him to Lexington when the trial is over, see if they can help him. I'm hoping winter won't be too bad and the snow holds off."

Joe let out a whistle. "That's a long trip, expensive too. How'd you manage that?"

Berl felt his cheeks flushing. "We've been saving. Plus I've been doing some odd jobs. I'm a pretty handy fella, you know?" He grinned at Joe hoping to hide his discomfort.

"Yes, sir. You are that. Well, I just wanted to check on y'all and see if you needed anything. I hope those doctors in Lexington can help your son."

"Thank you, sheriff. So do I."

Joe gave him a knowing look and walked back to where Bullet was grazing. This wasn't looking good for Billy Akers.

# CHAPTER 20

"How are you feeling about court today?" Joe handed Billy his breakfast and pulled up a chair. Billy was expected to take the stand this morning and Joe wanted to try one last time to get the answers he needed.

"I feel good." Billy had nothing more to say in between bites. The thought of testifying was dampening his appetite.

"That's good, Billy. That's real good. I went to Owsley County over the weekend. I ran into your in-laws."

Billy stopped eating. "Why did you do that? Did you see Mattie? Leave my wife alone, sheriff."

Joe was taken aback by Billy's defensiveness. "I did not see Mattie. What I did see were two parents trying their best to protect their daughter. What are they protecting her from, Billy?"

"Me. They are protecting her from me."

"Why? Are you dangerous?"

"No. But, I'm an Akers and that puts her in danger. It puts me in danger. Mattie is where she needs to be. I can't let her get involved in this feud. Her folks are doing the right thing. Leave them alone."

"If Matilda knows something, Billy, then…"

"She doesn't know anything. Leave her be."

Joe sat and looked at Billy. The look of defiance on his face was far different than his usually easy-going demeanor. Joe had run out of options. Without talking to Matilda and with Billy not cooperating, he could only hope that the Caudills had not already decided Billy's fate.

"I hope you know what you're doing. You'll be on the stand today. That's probably your last chance to save yourself." Joe shook his head and walked outside. He needed some fresh air. Judge Wilson was arriving at the courthouse. Joe approached him as he was hitching his horse.

"Good morning, Joe. Any luck locating Matilda Akers in Owsley County?"

"No, unfortunately. I saw her parents and they both claim that she is with family elsewhere but wouldn't tell me where. I believe they might be lying, hard to say. They didn't like me being around that's for sure. I do want to make you aware of a conversation I had with Bob Akers. He seems to think that the Caudills have paid off a juror. I thought he was being paranoid, but I ran into Thomas Brewer Saturday and he had a whole load of goods from the store. It was way more than he could afford."

Judge Wilson was visibly worried. "That's odd. How did he come up with the money for that?"

"That's what I would like to know. I also went by Berl Adams's place to check on his boy and discovered that when the trial is over, they are taking him to Lexington to see if the doctors there can help him"

"Lexington? That's a big trip. How can they afford to travel to Lexington?"

"He claims he did some work…for Dan Caudill."

The judge stood contemplating what he just heard. That coincidence was dangerously close to the accusation made by Bob. "I don't like it, Joe. I don't like it one bit."

Joe agreed. "It could be innocent, but it seems strange. They are good men, both of them. But they are in bad situations. It makes me nervous."

"Me too. I'll remind the jury in court today of their duty. We need to keep an eye on them."

"Already on it. Thank you, Judge. I just wanted to let you know. I'll see you in court."

As Joe headed back to the jail to prepare his prisoner for his court date, Berl Adams was riding in. Bob Akers was standing in front of the bank watching. As Berl dismounted, Bob caught his eye. Berl's blood ran cold.

"Good mornin', Bob." He couldn't let Bob see the fear he was feeling.

"Good mornin', Berl. How's your boy?"

"Not well, actually. Thank you for asking."

"Hate to hear that. Seems we are both worrying about our sons these days." Berl could feel the piercing glare of Bob Akers on him.

"Yes, it appears we are." Berl wanted to get away from Bob as quickly as he could. Did he know? How could that be? The panic was starting to overwhelm him.

"Not sure there is anything more painful for a man than losing his son, especially if he doesn't deserve it. Both our boys are suffering an injustice at the same time. What are the odds, huh? Makes a man want to do desperate things to save them. Doesn't it, Berl?"

Berl could feel himself trembling. Could Bob see it, too? "Yes, I imagine so, Bob. A man certainly wants to protect his own. I better get into the courthouse. Good seeing you, Bob."

"Yes. I'll see you inside, Berl." Bob's eyes never left Berl as he watched him enter the courthouse.

Bob's gaze was interrupted by the sound of shuffling behind him. He turned to see Rondal Gross slowly making his way to court. "How are you doing, Rondal?"

"Well, my back hurts but there ain't nothin' I can do about that I reckon. I don't know a farmer around that don't have a bad back. Heading in here to sit on those old hard jury seats." Rondal rarely had a positive thing to say.

Bob chuckled. "I sure hate to hear that. Maybe they'll start letting you bring a pillow."

"I doubt it. They don't want us gettin' too comfortable. I'll see you inside." The old man continued his slow trek to the jury box. Bob opened the door for him to enter. He may be a grumpy old fella, but he was a hard worker in his day and deserved respect.

Joe unlocked the jail cell and proceeded to handcuff Billy for the walk to the courthouse. "Time to go, Billy. Today is your big day."

"I'm ready, sheriff." Billy felt no fear. He had been dreaming of Matilda and their child running through the grass. He was sure things would work out. Matilda was safe and he knew he was innocent. Justice would prevail.

Matilda had not left her bed in days. Mama was worried. She had offered her meals but they sat untouched. She felt helpless in how she could help her daughter. Sometimes she just sat in the room with her rocking and sewing while she reminisced about the good memories. Nothing changed Mattie's mental state. If she wasn't sleeping, she was staring straight ahead out the window. But mostly, she slept.

Matilda was numb. How did everything go so wrong? She was imprisoned in her parents' home with no idea how to escape. She had lied to Billy about the baby. She had been so close to being able to get to Sheriff Lawson and tell him everything. It didn't matter what that meant; if the Caudills wanted to kill her, if the whole town wanted to judge her, so be it. Life didn't feel worth the effort anymore. She was tired.
"All rise for the Honorable Jesse Wilson."

# CHAPTER 21

"Does the prosecution have any other witnesses?"

"No, Your Honor. Prosecution rests."

"Alright then. The defense may call its first witness."

Everett Thompson stood and faced the judge. "The defense would like to call William Akers to the stand, Your Honor."

Billy stood and walked to the stand. He did not hear the whispers of the crowd or the gavel hammering down for order. Placing his hand on the Bible, he prayed for mercy for the lies he was about to tell the court. His focus was held on the job at hand which was to convince the jury that he indeed did not kill Frank Prewitt and to go home to his family. Everett Thompson slowly sauntered to the stand.

"Would you please state your name for the record?"

"William Akers, sir."

"Thank you. Now, Mr. Akers, would you please tell the court what happened on that cold, wintry day in December of last year?"

"Yes, sir. I was out hunting for small game, you know, rabbits and squirrels. As I was walking along, I saw something on the ground ahead that looked out of place. I approached it and saw that it was Frank Prewitt. I was shocked and if I were to be completely honest, I was scared, too. I couldn't figure out why he would be on my land except that someone must have brought him there. I'm not proud of this, but I thought it might have had something to do with the feud. I knew Frank was kin to the Caudills and so I decided to bury him. If some of my family had a part in this, I felt I needed to protect them. I know it was wrong but I just couldn't allow myself to get anyone in trouble. I dug a hole for him, but the ground was so frozen, I couldn't dig very deep. I did the best I could thinking I could come back after things thawed out and do a better job. Then ol' Jack dug up his head and well...now I'm here."

"I see, I see. So how well did you know Frank Prewitt?"

"He did work for me, mending my boots."

"Did the two of you have any disagreements or bad blood?"

Billy's mind took him back to the morning he found Mattie unconscious in a pool of her own blood. The sight of Frank's decapitated head in his living room. The news that their baby was gone. He looked at Everett without hesitation.

"No, sir."

"So you had no reason to kill him?"

Billy thought of the blood splatter covering the front room wall. How Mattie awoke in complete terror from her ordeal. How he fell to the floor in his woodshed weeping for the trauma caused to his beloved wife and the death of their long-awaited child.

"No, sir."

"Are you regretful, Billy?"

"I know what I did was against the law. I hate that I broke that law. But if Frank Prewitt died due to the feud the Caudills have with my family, I know he probably did something to one of my own. I know it was wrong, but I can't say I wouldn't do it again." Billy had practiced that to himself all night. He knew he had to make his story believable and to do that, he would have to appear less than innocent.

"No further questions, Your Honor."

Judge Wilson looked to Claude Graham. "Prosecution, your witness."

Claude approached the witness stand studying Billy. "Very noble of you, protecting your family and all."

"I wouldn't say noble."

"Were the claw marks on Frank Prewitt's face when you found him?"

"I...I didn't notice. I was too shocked, I guess."

"Well, I mean, you had to move the body, dig a hole for the body, carry the head somehow...at some point you must have noticed the claw marks on his face. Did you or did you not?"

Billy was feeling anxious. "Yes, now that you mention it, there were claw marks on his face."

"Thank you. Sheriff Lawson reported that the head was buried at the foot of the body. Why would you do that?"

Billy shifted uneasily in his seat. "Um, well, I figured he must have done something to hurt my family for someone to have retaliated like that. I was angry."

Claude thought about this for a moment. "Mmm-hmm. Mr. Akers, where is your wife currently?"

Billy did not like how this was going. "She is with family, where she is safe."

"As opposed to here? Supporting you?"

"She supports me. I just don't want her around all of this." Billy had to remind himself to breathe. He could not lose control of the situation. His life depended on it.

"That's a shame. I would love to hear what she has to say. Since she isn't here to talk to us, would you like to hear what I think?"

"I've already told you what happened..."

"This is what I think. I think you walked in on something. Maybe Frank Prewitt was hurting your wife or maybe, maybe they were having an affair..."

Billy felt his blood begin to boil.

"You walked into your house and caught them together in the throes of passion..."

Billy saw Matilda lying on the floor in her own blood.

"Your wife was betraying you, giving herself to another man..."

The courtroom erupted. Judge Wilson began banging his gavel. Everett Thompson stood up. "Objection! Calls for speculation!"

"Your wife and Frank Prewitt were caught in an illicit affair and in a fit of rage, you began attacking him physically.

The two of you were in a physical fight and your wife tried to pull you apart and ended up clawing Frank Prewitt's face in the scuffle..."

Billy was blind with rage.

"And with a mighty blow with the ax! You chopped off the head of your wife's lover!"

"You son of a bitch!" Billy charged at Claude Graham with such speed and fury that he had his hands around the attorney's throat before Sheriff Lawson and three other men could attempt to pull him off.

"I swear to God I will kill you! How dare you! I'll kill you! Do you hear me!?"

Everett Thompson had screamed his ignored objections. Now, he just stood shocked at what he witnessed. The courtroom was roaring as Judge Wilson was furiously banging his gavel. "Order in this court! I demand order! Sheriff take this man back to his cell. Claude! Everett! In my chambers immediately. Everyone out of this courtroom! Now!"

Joe handcuffed Billy and led him out the door to a holding cell. "You lost it, Billy. I don't blame you, but you lost it."

"He was out of line. There's no way I was going to sit there and let him talk about Mattie like that. He deserved what he got."

"That may be so, but it doesn't look good for you. Sit there and cool off."

Judge Wilson walked into his office and slammed the door as he looked at Claude and Everett sitting uncomfortably in wait. "What the hell do you call that Claude?! You were completely out of line in your questioning. Everett! Did you not prepare your client for cross-examination? This is a house of justice, not a circus tent! A man's life is in the balance here. You may not take that seriously, but I do! Claude, I will be striking your line of questioning from the record. Everett, get control of your client. Both of you, out of my office. We will reconvene at 2 p.m. Out!"

Joe let Everett into Billy's cell. He sat down on the cot next to his client. "I'm sorry, Billy. I should have prepared you for that. I didn't know he would go there, but my job is to prepare you for anything and...well...I failed. The judge is going to strike the remarks from the record and hopefully, the jury will see that Claude was in the wrong."

"I'll try to stay calm when we go back, but if he starts talking about Mattie again...I can't make any promises."

"I know. We know what to expect now. The judge will reconvene at 2. I will see you then."

At 2 p.m. the spectators began filing in. They did not want to miss the chance for another fight or news of a steamy affair. This was the most exciting thing that had happened in their town in years; it seemed everyone wanted to watch.

Billy sat quietly. He decided that he would think of their baby the next time Claude came at him. It was the only thing he could think of that might keep him from going after Claude Graham's throat.

"All rise for the Honorable Jesse Wilson."

Judge Wilson walked in and sat at his bench. "What I witnessed earlier was a shame and a travesty. I will not allow accusations based on speculation in my courtroom nor will I allow bar room brawls. The jury will strike not only the questioning by Claude Graham but also the comments and actions made by William Akers. With that being said, I believe it is in the best interest of all involved to call a recess until 9 a.m. tomorrow. Court is adjourned."

As the gavel came down, Berl and Thomas realized how easy their job was going to be.

# CHAPTER 22

When Billy took the stand the next morning, he was prepared for his cross-examination. He knew the outburst from yesterday damaged his chances. Now he could only hope that he could mend what was broken. Before Claude Graham approached the stand, he turned to the jury.

"Gentlemen of the jury, I owe you an apology. I speculated an idea that rightfully could have happened but without having evidence to back up my theory. This theory was completely circumstantial. In doing so, I caused a great deal of chaos in Judge Wilson's courtroom. For that, I am sorry. Now I will proceed with further questioning." He turned and approached Billy. "Billy, I would like to continue with the claw marks on Frank Prewitt's face. When you found the decapitated head of Mr. Prewitt, what did you think caused those injuries to his face?"

"I assumed it was an animal or something. I didn't really think about it."

"I see. Do you find it strange that an animal would scratch the flesh of a man's face without eating it? I mean, it's the dead of winter and the smell of fresh blood would be very tempting to say a bear or a coyote, don't you think?"

"I suppose."

"Here's what I think...now hear me out. I think that those claw marks occurred during some sort of scuffle. The scuffle became violent and an ax was used as a weapon. Prewitt died. I don't think that body ever laid outside. I think it was buried immediately afterward. Think about this Mr. Akers, what if the deceased was killed inside a home, for example, and then taken to be buried from there. That would explain why the flesh of the victim wasn't eaten by an animal. It had never laid out in the open air to draw any in. Isn't that possible?"

"I don't know about any of that. I found…"

"Yes, I know. You say you found him while you were out hunting, I know. I just wanted to share that with you. I thought with you being such a smart hunter, that you would find that as fascinating as I did. I wish your wife was here so I could share it with her, too. No further questions."

Billy felt stunned. He could feel the darkness circling him. Everett Thompson stood up.

"Your honor, may I be allowed to redirect?"

"Proceed."

"Billy, did you kill Frank Prewitt?"

"No, sir."

"Billy, did your wife, Matilda Akers, kill Frank Prewitt?"

With the image of the carnage that he had found in his home, Billy locked eyes with Claude Graham.

"No, sir."

"No further questions, Your Honor."

Judge Wilson turned to Billy. "You may step down, son. Claude, you may give your closing arguments."

Billy sat next to Everett Thompson wishing he could go home.

Matilda had stayed in bed for several days without eating. She no longer cared about her future, it had been decided against her will. The longer she lay in bed, the more the rage in her grew, the more the resentment began to mount. The only way to deal with her emotions was to sleep. She had decided that if she died in that bed, she was ready. Death would be a comfort at this point. It wasn't until her mother came in one night before bed, choking back tears, "Mattie, I'm sorry about all of this. I am. We were just trying to protect you, but this is wrong and I know it's wrong. My hands are tied, sweetheart. Please, get out of bed in the morning and eat breakfast with me." She left Mattie lying in her bed, a tear slowly rolled down her cheek.

The next morning, Mattie waited until her father had left to do his farm work. She pulled herself out of the bed, her joints stiff and painful from lack of movement. She put on a clean dress and joined her mother in the kitchen. Mama looked at her with a sad smile and began fixing her a plate. Neither spoke, but there was an understanding. Mattie knew that Mama would support her. She would need her help.

Mattie began going through the motions of doing chores and getting into a routine. She only spoke to her father when spoken to. She spent most days in silence, solemnly getting through each day. The color had come back into her cheeks but her smile was erased. Her only goal was to find where Daddy kept the keys to the stall padlocks. She watched his every move. The keys were never out of his sight. But one day he would slip and Mattie would be waiting.

It wasn't long before Mama began inviting Mattie to come along on her trips to town. She hoped that being a part of the community again would revive the old Mattie that had been missing for so long. With the sheriff long gone and Mattie taking part in the running of the family farm, this might be just the thing to bring back the daughter she once knew. Mattie knew otherwise.

Mattie and Mama were picking up goods at the store when Mr. Hobbs pulled out a letter from behind the register. "Mrs. Mattie, you received a letter a few days ago. I was hoping you would come by." Mattie felt the electricity surge through her body. She had not heard from Billy and was both excited and terrified by what was inside. Mama had been out of earshot so Mattie hid the letter in her dress.

"Thank you, Mr. Hobbs." The friendly storekeeper smiled and went back to his work. Mattie would read the letter privately later.

After unloading the wagon and putting things away, Mama got busy preparing supper while Mattie went to the chicken coop. Daddy had gone hunting and wouldn't be back until evening. Once she was safely out of sight, Mattie opened the letter. As she read, her heart sank.

*November 30, 1849*

*My Dearest Matilda,*

*I hope this letter finds you safe and well. I think of you and the baby continuously. I wish I could see you and your growing belly. You are where you need to be, my love. I wish I was writing with better news. Claude Graham has made accusations that tarnish your name and dignity. Because of this, I lost my temper and attacked the man in court. Had they not pulled me off of him, I surely would have killed him. Although he and the judge have told those in the courtroom that his accusations are pure speculation, the townspeople are murmuring. If by some miracle I can come home to you, I want to leave Clay County and go as far away from it as we can. I want our family to have a fresh start.*
*I fear that this is not going to turn out well. Daddy thinks that the Caudills have paid off jurors and my outburst has not helped the situation. I still hope that justice will prevail, but I want you to make a plan for you and the baby, just in case. Your safety is what matters.*

*I love you, Matilda, with all of my heart. I love our baby, too. If this doesn't go our way, be sure to tell him or her that every day so that they know.*

*Your loving husband,*

*Billy*

    Mattie leaned against the cold boards of the chicken coop and read the letter again, her hand on her empty womb. She had to get to Clay County and talk to the sheriff, the judge, whoever would listen. She didn't care what folks were saying. She knew the truth.

    Mattie hid the letter and finished her chores. She sat down to supper and ate in silence. Every move her father made was made under her watchful eye. She would escape this prison and get to Billy. She had to.

    After closing arguments, Judge Wilson released the jurors

to the back room. Berl Adams spoke up immediately, "Let's take a vote before we get started. How many find Billy Akers guilty?"

Berl and Thomas raised their hands, along with six others.

"Innocent?"

Rondal Gross raised his hand.

"Undecided?"

Eugene Bush, Lee Campbell, and John Sizemore raised their hands.

"Hmph. Looks like we just have four to convince."

Rondal Gross looked at them defiantly. "You won't convince me of nothin'!"

# CHAPTER 23

"Old man, how could you actually believe that he didn't do it?" Berl was shocked. He hadn't expected Rondal to vote Billy as innocent. "Were we in the same courtroom??"

Rondal's gaze never wavered as he looked straight into the eyes of Berl Adams. "There is nothing that they said in that there courtroom that proves Billy Akers did anything except'n hide that body. Nothin'! I'm not sure why you're so fired up to hang him!"

Berl felt a rush of guilt that he swiftly cast aside. He remembered his son's tired body lying in his wife's arms as he left that morning. "Well, if he didn't do it, then who did?"

"Any of the Akers could have. Hell, I'd say there are several folks that would have killed him. Frank Prewitt was a good cobbler, but he was a son of a bitch."

Thomas decided he needed to earn his bribe. It helped to know that Berl thought Billy was guilty already. "Well, I think Billy did it. Seems too convenient that he just happened upon a body like that. Why would the Akers put a body on his land? They wouldn't frame one of their own. Even a weaker one like Billy."

Rondal spoke up. "You just proved my point, Thomas. Billy ain't the killin' kind. He's stayed out of the feud and has avoided all conflict. Now, he decides to cut a man's head off?? Doesn't make any sense. No way Bob would let anyone frame his son. Ridiculous! I'll say this, though, Tom. Avoiding a fight that doesn't make sense doesn't make you weak. Too many have died in that feud."

Thomas felt like a schoolboy being corrected by his

teacher. "I still think he did it."

"What about his wife?" Everyone turned to look at John Sizemore. "She's disappeared. Nobody has seen her for months. Maybe she did it. Claude's argument made a lot of sense to me."

"We're not supposed to consider that." Berl was worried that he would lose control of the jury. If he wasn't able to secure a guilty verdict, he wasn't sure what that would mean for his son. "The judge told us not to use it."

"I don't give a damn what the judge said." John was obviously annoyed with Berl's self-nomination as the leader. "A man can't unhear what was said and I say it makes sense." The rest of the jurors began murmuring and nodding their heads in agreement.

"You tryin' to tell me that little woman cut off Frank's head. You've lost your mind. Now, I will get behind the idea that she was having an affair and Billy caught them and that HE killed Frank Prewitt." Berl was proud of himself for redirecting the jurors to return their focus on Billy.

Rondal guffawed. "Matilda Akers is one of the prettiest women in town. She wouldn't touch Frank Prewitt with a ten-foot pole. That's the craziest thing I've ever heard! Both of you should be ashamed for discussing that anyway. The judge said not to, so we won't."

"Oh, shut up, you ol' coot." Berl had hoped this would be easier.

Mattie knew that she was running out of time. She had to talk to her mother. Surely, she will understand the desperation she was feeling. She waited until Daddy was out on a long hunting trip to approach the subject.

"Mama, I know you don't agree with me, but I have to find a way to get to Clay County. I have to tell the truth to the sheriff about what happened to me. I can't let Billy take the fall for something that I did out of self-defense. I had to kill Frank Prewitt, Mama, or he would have killed me."

"Matilda, we have been over this. My hands are tied."

"Mama, I just need some advice."

Mama looked at her daughter and saw the pleading in her eyes. Her heart broke for her. The fact was she no longer knew what was the right thing to do. It had all gotten so twisted somehow.

"I wish I knew what to tell you. It's not easy being a woman, Matilda. A man can have his way with us, rape us, beat us, yet we are expected to make it stop or just take it. Somehow we deserved it. It's wrong. Your daddy is afraid that you will get charged with murder or that the Caudills will come after you. Even if that doesn't happen, you will be marked for the rest of your life. You'll be the talk of the town, they'll say all kinds of awful things about you. He can't stand the idea of that. I know you want to help Billy. Sheriff Lawson is a just man; I doubt he would charge you with murder. I just have a feeling about that. The Akers have a plan, Matilda, believe it."

"I can't let him die, Mama."

"Stop saying that. He's not going to die."

"Mama, he sent me a letter. He wants me to prepare for the worst. I need your help."

Mama saw the tears in Mattie's eyes. She had been telling herself that the Akers would figure this out, that they would take care of their own. Now it seemed that Billy Akers's blood could be on her hands.

"I see. I don't know what to say." She appeared lost in thought. "I will tell you this. You kill more flies with honey than with vinegar. Think about that the next time you talk to your daddy."

Mattie knew exactly what she meant. She needed to win her father's trust for him to let his guard down. He had to believe she wasn't going to run.

Before the jury went home for the night, Berl took another vote...nine guilty, two undecideds, and one not guilty. He was getting closer. He needed to come up with a plan to convince the three to change their vote. Rondal was going to be the biggest challenge. Berl approached Thomas after they had been released.

"Thanks for backing me up in there. I guess if we can get the other three to see it our way, we can be done with this, huh?"

"Yessir, but that Rondal, he's a tough old bird."

"That he is. Look, Tom, I really need your help tomorrow. This verdict, well, it's important."

"It's important to me, too. Very important."

The two men looked at each other. They both understood what was on the line. They also understood that they were in this together.

Joe took Billy's dinner plate away. He hadn't touched it. He had not said a word since coming back to the jail. He spent most of the day sleeping. Billy was losing hope.

# CHAPTER 24

Matilda could see in the distance her father riding back from his hunting trip. As he got closer, she noticed that he had brought back a deer. This was her opportunity to attempt to regain his trust, and in turn, her freedom. As he rode Tucker up to the barn, Matilda walked out to meet him.

"Looks like you had a good hunt. Would you like some help preparing the meat?"

George was surprised to hear Mattie speaking to him. "Oh, um, yes. Yes, that would be good if you could give me a hand."

Mattie helped him unload the deer. It had already been field-dressed. She took it inside the barn to prepare the individual cuts. As she sharpened her knife and began separating the muscles and joints, she was aware of Daddy approaching Tucker's stall. She pretended not to notice but was set on figuring out where he kept the key. She saw him unbutton the top button of his shirt and pull up a necklace of twine with two keys dangling from them. How on earth would she ever get those from around his neck?? She continued slicing the deer meat into cutlets, pretending to take no notice of what her father was doing.

"Would you like for me to take these deer steaks in for Mama to prepare, Daddy?"

"Yes, that would be good. I like to celebrate a good hunt with a good meal."

"I've got enough here to take to her. I'll get them inside and come back to finish this up."

George was still taken aback by Matilda speaking. "Thank you, Mattie. I'll finish this up. You help your mother."

Mattie smiled and took the meat into the house. As she walked away, she realized that saving Billy felt farther away than ever.

The jury filed into the room early the next morning. Berl had been awake all night planning how he could gain the three votes needed for a conviction. He decided that he needed to approach the case with steady persistence which he hoped would pay off.

"Let's start today by looking at the evidence again." Berl wanted to get things rolling quickly.

All eyes were on Berl as he prepared his presentation of the evidence that was introduced to them.

"We know that Billy buried the body. He admitted to that. We also know he buried the head of Frank Prewitt at his feet as a show of disrespect. He admitted to that, too"

The jurors nodded and murmured in agreement.

"Sheriff Lawson found blood splatter on the ceiling of Billy's house. He also found a potato sack at their home that matches the one used to carry Frank's head. An ax was found stored in the same room as the blood splatter."

Again, the jurors nodded in agreement.

"You're forgetting the scratches on his face." John Sizemore was not going to let go of his theory that Matilda may have killed Frank Prewitt.

"Could have been made by an animal." Rondal rebutted.

"The face scratches don't mean a thing. Take the face scratches out of it. Why would there be bloodstains on Billy Akers's ceiling? We all know he didn't slaughter a pig in his living room!" Berl was losing patience and time. This trial needed to be over so that he could get his family to Lexington before the winter snows hit.

"That's a good point, Berl." Thomas was impressed by Berl's quick thinking. Supporting him seemed to be the safest way to fulfill his end of the bargain with the Caudills.

"I still say those claw marks are important." John couldn't let go of his theory. "Matilda Akers disappearing along with that seems suspicious to me."

"She may have left out of shame, John. The shame of being caught by her husband in a love affair with Frank Prewitt." Berl was determined to get a guilty verdict.

"Ridiculous!" Rondal was not convinced.

Berl could tell that John was considering his theory. Rondal was going to be a much more difficult hurdle.

"Listen, old man. I know that you think Matilda couldn't have had an affair with Frank Prewitt, but where the hell is she? Why isn't she here supporting her husband? Huh?"

Rondal stared stone-faced at Berl. "I don't know and I don't care. What you are doing is called speculation and that is NOT what we are supposed to be doin'" The old man crossed his arms and remained firm in his stance. Berl knew more drastic measures may be necessary to change the stubborn man's mind.

"Let's take another vote and see where we stand. Raise your hand if you think Billy Akers is guilty."

Ten hands went up. Berl looked at John Sizemore who seemed undecided. "John?" Slowly, John raised his hand.

"Innocent?"

Rondal Gross raised his hand defiantly. That would change after tonight.

Matilda and her family enjoyed the deer steaks that Daddy had brought home with some fried potatoes and cornbread. She and her mother got up to clean off the table as Daddy was getting up to go sit in his chair and smoke his pipe.

"That was a delicious meal, Mama. Next time you go hunting Daddy maybe I could go with you. It's been a while."

George was visibly shocked. "Um, yes. Yes, that would be nice, Mattie. We'll plan on that." He didn't know what to make of this change in his daughter, but it was a pleasant surprise. Mattie nodded and continued helping her mother.

Mattie lay in bed that night contemplating how to get the padlock keys from around Daddy's neck. She would have to earn his trust to the point he no longer needed the padlocks anymore. That would take too much time. Until she could come up with another plan, she would have to keep moving forward with this one. She closed her eyes and said a prayer for her Billy.

As the sun rose, Rondal prepared his breakfast. The jury was meeting at 9 a.m. Bacon, eggs, and biscuits should hold him. He had become quite the cook since his beloved Liza had passed. The house and farm could get lonely. They never had any children, so it was just him and his hound dog, Blue. Yes, it was lonely, but it was peaceful.

Getting dressed he thought of how Berl was so determined to convict Billy Akers. It was beyond him as to why he wanted to watch a man hang if there was a possibility that he was innocent. Rondal couldn't figure out his motive but it didn't matter. Billy's blood wasn't going to be on his hands. He would stand for what he believed in.

Rondal grabbed his hat along with a biscuit and slice of bacon that he put back for his dog. He opened the door to his cabin. The biscuit dropped to the floor as he stared down in disbelief at the severed head of his dear companion, Blue.

# CHAPTER 25

Bob Akers sat quietly next to the lifeless body of his beloved. Sarah had been ill for months but had recently taken a turn for the worse. As dawn broke over the hills surrounding their home, she gave up her fight. Bob knew that as the sun continued to rise, he would need to speak with Marcus and begin preparations for her burial. But for now, he just wanted to sit beside her a little while longer in the peaceful quiet of the morning.

Joe cleared the breakfast dishes at the jail, Billy barely touched his food these days. It was understandable considering the uncertainty that lay ahead. "You need to eat, Billy. No use starving yourself before the verdict is even read."

"I'm not hungry. Thank you."

Joe said nothing but continued cleaning up when Bob Akers walked in. "Good morning, Bob. How are you doin'?"

Bob looked tired. "Sheriff, do you mind if I talk to Billy for a minute...privately?"

"Sure, sure, I'll be back here if you need me. I hope everything is alright." The look on Bob's face answered that question without words. "Take your time."

Billy looked at his father, concerned. He knew his mother had been ill recently, but he was also concerned for Matilda and the baby. "What's wrong?"

Bob pulled up a chair and sat down. "I guess the best way to tell you is to just come out with it. Your mama passed this morning. She just couldn't fight anymore. I just met with Marcus to take care of the burial. I'll speak with Joe to see if you can attend the funeral."

Billy's heart sank. "I'm sure I will be joining her soon. The jury is on day three of deliberation. I'm as good as dangling from the rope."

"She wouldn't want to hear you talk like that. I don't want to hear it either. She loved you, son."

"I know." Billy stared at the floor; everything felt surreal.

Bob got up and went to the back where Joe was taking care of his morning duties. "Sheriff, Billy's mama passed this morning. Would he be allowed to attend the funeral?"

"I'm so sorry to hear that, Bob. Yes, of course. I'll have to accompany him, but just let me know when and we'll be there. You have my condolences, Bob. Sarah was a good lady."

"She was...that she was. Thank you, sheriff."

Jury members had begun arriving at the courthouse. Bob stepped out of the sheriff's office and surveyed the day. He noticed a small figure coming up the road with a slight limp. Rondal Gross was walking faster than Bob had seen him move in years. The look on his face showed that he was beyond his usual sour disposition. He was angry. Berl was standing outside the courthouse. Rondal was heading straight toward him.

"You! You son of a bitch!" Rondal's long twisted finger was pointing at Berl. "You won't get away with this!"

Berl looked at him coolly. Bob took a seat on the bench outside the jail. No one had noticed his presence. He wanted to know what had been going on behind those jury doors. Rondal was right under Berl's nose.

"You killed my dog. I know it was you. You want to threaten me, Berl?! I'm too close to meeting my maker to be scared of you."

Berl looked down at the angry old man. "What are you talkin' about you crazy old coot? You've lost your mind."

"Don't play dumb with me, Berl Adams. You killed my dog and I know it."

Berl hadn't killed Blue, but he had spoken with Thomas about doing something to shake up Rondal to change his vote. Thomas had said he had an idea. Berl was both shocked and impressed.

"I don't know what you're talking about. But it seems to me, whoever is mad at you was giving you a warning. Whatever happened to Blue, might be getting ready to happen to you." His eyes never left Rondal's angry gaze. "You might be meeting that maker of yours quicker than you think."

Rondal stood his ground as they stared at each other. "You son of a bitch." He made his way to the courthouse, slamming the door behind him. Berl watched him enter and gave a chuckle to himself.

"Damn, Thomas."

Berl had been so focused on Rondal, he never heard the approaching footsteps. He was still watching the courthouse when a voice broke his thoughts.

"Hey there, Berl."

Berl turned around to face Bob Akers's fist on his jaw. He fell to the ground looking up at the father of Billy Akers.

"I'll see you in hell, Berl Adams." Bob turned and walked back toward his wagon. He knew without question who was leading the jury for the Caudills. He would deal with him later; for now, he needed to bury his wife.

Word of Billy's trial had made it to Owsley County. Mattie's trips to town were now full of dread as the town folk would want to ask questions or look at her with pity. She had overheard her mother telling Mrs. Preston at the store, "We told her marrying an Akers from Clay County was a bad idea but she was determined." None of them knew her Billy. Their judgment angered her.

Mattie had been working on gaining her father's trust, but progress was moving too slow. She had noticed Ira watching her when he didn't think she knew. It was obvious that he found her attractive. But he never disrespected the fact that she was a married woman. Ira may hold the key to her escape.

She and Mama were getting supplies at Mr. Hobbs's store. Mama was enjoying a conversation with one of her friends allowing Mattie to speak privately with Ira.

"Mama, I'm going to step outside and put these in the

wagon." Mama smiled and continued her conversation.

Ira was putting a new coat of paint on the front porch. "Good morning, Ira. You seem to be working hard."

Ira was surprised by the interruption. "Good morning, Miss Mattie. Yes, I guess you could say that. Here, I will help you load your wagon." Ira quickly began gathering Mattie's packages to load.

"Um...I heard about your husband in Clay County. I'm sorry to hear about what you are going through. Are you doing okay?"

Mattie was moved by Ira's kindness. "Not really, Ira. People think he is guilty because of his family and the feud. He's innocent and I know it. I need to get to the sheriff to tell him what I know. It could save him, but my daddy has me trapped here."

Ira was listening intently. "Trapped?"

"Yes, he has the horses locked up and I can't go anywhere by myself. He is worried about me; that's why he's doing it. Doesn't make it right, though. An innocent man could hang, Ira. That's just wrong!" Mattie felt a lump in her throat at the thought of this.

"My goodness, Mattie. That's awful. I'm sorry."

"Ira, may I ask you, do you have any horses?"

"Why, yes, back in Virginia. My uncle has a couple, though, and there's the one I rode in on. His name is Buck."

"Is Buck fast?"

"Oh, yes! He is a really fast horse. I trained him myself."

Mattie was seeing an opening. She could see her Mama just inside the door. She didn't have much time.

"Ira, I may need your help. I will talk to you next week, okay?"

"Sure, Miss Mattie, absolutely."

Mama stepped out and began walking toward the wagon. Mattie was waiting. "Sorry, Mattie, I hadn't seen Mrs. Johnson for so long. It was nice to catch up. Hello, Ira. Thank you for loading the wagon. We'll see you next week."

"Yes, ma'am. Have a nice day."

Mama boarded the wagon and clucked to the horses. She did not notice the smile of defiance resting on Mattie's face.

# CHAPTER 26

John Sizemore and Thomas were sitting quietly in the jury room awaiting everyone's arrival when Rondal Gross stormed into the room. The agitated old man's jerky movements and uneven breathing concerned John. Thomas knew what was wrong.

"Are you ok, old man?" John asked, concerned.

"No! No, I'm not ok! Somebody killed my dog! I found his head on my porch this morning. It was Berl Adams as sure as I'm sittin' here. I know it! I'm not swaying my vote. I won't be intimidated I'm telling you...I won't!"

Thomas moved over closer to Rondal, appearing to want to help the situation. "Now, Rondal. Berl may disagree with you, but he's not a bad person. You know that. Those are some strong accusations you're throwing around."

"He's right." John chimed in. "I have a hard time seeing Berl doing something like that. I can't imagine anyone in this jury doing that if you want to hear the truth. Now the Caudills? That's another story. If word got out that you were the one vote that is keeping Billy Akers from a conviction, well, they might be sending you a message."

Rondal sat contemplating that idea for a moment. "It was Berl. I know it was Berl."

Thomas shifted uneasily and leaned in closer to Rondal. "I don't believe Berl would do that, but whoever it was is sending you a message. What if you are next, Rondal?"

"That's true. Somebody is giving you a warning." John was visibly worried about the old man's safety.

"That's not right. I feel how I feel. Threatening me won't change that."

"Look Rondal," John spoke genuinely, "I know you feel strongly about this. But is it worth dying over? Eleven of us see it differently. Just because you disagree or see it differently doesn't make you right."

"What if it's YOUR head next time, Rondal?" Thomas was thankful for John's unknowing assistance.

Rondal sat with this quietly. He looked down at his hands and said nothing. Berl walked in, wiping his bloody nose with a handkerchief.

"What happened to you??" John was wondering what the hell was going on this morning.

"I tripped and fell outside." Berl lied. "Listen here you old coot. I didn't kill your damn dog."

Rondal didn't look up. "I don't believe you." He spoke quietly, looking defeated. All four men sat waiting for the rest of the jury in silence.

Matilda was preparing for the last trip to town before Christmas. She continued to work with her father attempting to win back his trust to no avail. Her keys to freedom remained dangling around his neck. Her only hope was for Ira to allow her to borrow his horse. Time was of the essence. She needed to clear Billy's name and her conscience. She had to tell Billy the truth about her pregnancy. So much was riding on this visit.

As she and Mama pulled their wagon up to the front of the store, Mattie had to contain her anxiousness. She couldn't tip her mother off to her plans. It was obvious that Mama had mixed feelings about Matilda's need to leave town, but the trip would be dangerous to travel alone. There was no doubt that she would try to stop her. Mattie's goal was to talk to Ira and get everything set up without Mama's knowledge.

They walked into the store and began picking up the items needed for their Christmas dinner. Mattie scanned the area looking for Ira. He was nowhere to be found. Mr. Hobbs was busily stocking the shelves. Matilda maneuvered her way near him.

"Good morning, Mr. Hobbs. You look mighty busy this

morning."

Mr. Hobbs turned and smiled broadly at Matilda. "Oh, yes! Christmas is a busy time of year here, that's for sure. That and my help has gone home for Christmas."

Mattie's heart sank. She tried to hide her deep disappointment at the news Ira was out of town. "So Ira has gone back to Virginia for the holiday I assume?" She hoped Mr. Hobbs did not detect the trembling in her voice.

"Yes, he'll be back after the first of the year. I'm not sure though; he doesn't seem content working in a store. I think he would prefer to be a farmer. I'll have to wait and see."

Mattie felt a panic arise within her. "Are you thinking he won't come back?"

"I don't know. I think he will come back, but I'm not sure how long he will stay. He may surprise me. I have a couple of other nephews that might be interested. I'm getting older and need to think about who I will hand this over to seeing as I never had children of my own. Too busy here to think about a family. I guess you could say the store is like my child." Mr. Hobbs looked around proudly.

"Yes, I imagine so." Mattie was feeling hopelessness settling in. "Well, I should let you get back to work. I need to finish this shopping list! I hope you have a Merry Christmas, Mr. Hobbs." Mattie attempted to sound cheerful.

"And you as well, Mrs. Mattie. Thank you very much." Mr. Hobbs smiled and went back to his work. Mattie had managed to hide her emotions from him but she wasn't sure how long she could hide them from Mama. She busied herself with the task at hand and tried not to think about her plans being changed yet again.

On their way home, Matilda could no longer hold back the tears. She quietly allowed them to stream down her cheeks. Mama took notice.

"Why, Matilda. What is wrong? Are you crying?"

"Yes, ma'am. I'm just worried about Billy. I haven't heard from him and it's Christmas time. I'm just missing him, I guess.

I'm terribly worried."

Mama said nothing. There was nothing she could say.

With all of the jurors present, Berl decided to start with a vote to see where they were in the process. "Let's take a vote and then we'll start discussing afterward. How many find Billy Akers innocent of the crime of murder?"

No one raised their hand. Berl felt his heart begin to race. "How many find him guilty?" All but Rondal Gross raised their hand. "Rondal?"

Rondal had not looked up. The vision of his beloved dog Blue's head on his front porch haunted him. He knew that Berl was the most likely suspect to have done it. Thomas had made a good point that it might have been one of the Caudills if they had gotten word that he was the holdout vote. He was torn between standing by his convictions and fearing for what might happen to him if he caused a mistrial. He was not a man afraid to die. He was, however, frightened of the idea of being tortured. A person who could kill a dog like Blue could do some evil things to a man. He closed his eyes and said a silent prayer and slowly raised his head to meet the gaze of Berl Adams.

"Guilty."

# CHAPTER 27

"C'mon Billy, we got to go. They have reached a verdict." Sheriff Lawson opened the cell door and prepared to cuff Billy for the walk to the courthouse. Billy said nothing. He knew what the verdict would be; he felt it in his bones.

As the two walked through town, Billy ignored the stares of the people preparing to enter. He only thought of Matilda and the baby. He longed to see her just one more time, to meet his child and watch it grow. He entered the courtroom stoic, prepared for his fate.

Matilda had been unable to focus on any of the holiday preparations. Mama was planning a large Christmas feast for visiting family. She had hoped that the holiday festivities might take Mattie's mind off of Billy's legal trouble and her obsession with going to Clay County to speak with Sheriff Lawson. Mama wished Mattie would put that part of her life behind her. George was adamant that they keep her at the home place to protect her. There was no convincing him otherwise. Mattie spent most of her days distracted in thought. Mama did not realize that Mattie had a plan that hinged completely on the return of Ira from Virginia. Mattie loved Christmas, but this year, she could not wait for the holidays to be over.

Bob Akers had been coming to town daily to see if a verdict had been reached. As he rode into town, he saw Ramah Booth walking toward him.

"They're holding court at 1 o'clock. The jury has reached a verdict. Thought you would want to know."

"Thanks, Ramah. I appreciate it."

"Anytime, Bob. I wish you and Billy the best." Ramah patted Bob's horse and tried to force a reassuring smile. But they both knew the odds were stacked against his soft-spoken son.

Bob sat waiting in the courtroom. As Sheriff Lawson escorted Billy to his chair, Bob could not help but notice the blankness in Billy's face. He could see that his son had lost hope for justice to prevail. For a moment, Bob was relieved that Sarah was not here to see this. He hoped that Heaven would protect her from witnessing it.

Dan and Charles Caudill waited expectantly for the verdict. They had kept their distance from Tom and Berl to alleviate suspicion. Both men sat hoping that the family investment had paid off.

Joe Lawson sat behind Billy. Something still felt completely wrong. He was missing something but could not put his finger on it. As he surveyed the courtroom, the smug looks of Dan and Charles Caudill left him uneasy. He wanted to believe that the jury had not been tainted, for Billy's sake.

The jury filed in. Tom and Berl held their heads high. Rondal appeared ill. The looks on the twelve faces did not indicate the announcement of good news. Judge Wilson came out of his chambers and approached the bench.

"All rise for the Honorable Judge Jesse Wilson."

Judge Wilson sat down and faced the jury. "So, have you reached a verdict?"

Berl Adams stood up. "We have, Your Honor." He handed the verdict to the bailiff.

"What say ye?"

Billy closed his eyes in preparation.

"We the jury find the defendant, William Akers, guilty of the murder of Frank Prewitt."

The courtroom roared with shock and chatter. Judge Wilson pounded his gavel and demanded order. Bob Akers dropped his head. Dan and Charles smiled.

"Would the defendant please stand?"

Billy stood and looked directly into the eyes of Judge Wilson.

"William Akers, you have been found guilty of the crime of murder. It is hereby decided by this court in accordance with the laws of the Commonwealth of Kentucky that you shall be hanged for your crime. The hanging will take place in front of the courthouse on December 30, 1850. May God have mercy on your soul. This court is adjourned."

Sheriff Lawson quickly escorted Billy away. The crowd filed out of the courtroom discussing the excitement of this recent event. The jury began to file out, relieved that this was over. All but one. Rondal Gross could not take his eyes off of Bob Akers as he sat motionless, looking at his hands.

Billy lay that night in his cell staring at the night sky. Christmas was days away and light snow was beginning to fall. The full moon reflected off of the flakes as they gently floated down. Billy gazed at the scene with a soft smile across his face. He was not devastated by his fate. He was at peace. Soon, he will see his mother at the heavenly gates, his wife is safe and his child will carry on his legacy. This is the will of God and he would accept it. He closed his eyes as tears slowly rolled down his cheeks.

# CHAPTER 28

Mattie had not slept for days. Christmas was arriving soon and all she could think of was getting to Billy, to Sheriff Lawson, to getting back to her old life. Her empty womb filled her with guilt. The memories of that horrible night with Frank Prewitt haunted her. She could not allow Billy to die for the evil that Prewitt caused. She had a glimmer of hope in Ira's kindness and generosity. On horseback, she could arrive in Clay County in just a few hours. Salvation for her husband was only a few hours away, yet she was trapped under the overprotectiveness of her parents. A prisoner in her own right. The waiting was torture and the idea of the fate that may await Billy was unbearable.

She had spent the previous week preparing for the visit of the family for the holiday. She had feigned a smile in hopes of her father letting down his guard and removing the coveted keys to the horse stalls from around his neck. Much to her frustration, he had not. Mattie tried speaking to her mother about visiting Billy for Christmas, but she would not hear of it. Her future felt hopeless with each passing day. If only Ira would get back from Virginia and her plans could come to fruition.

"Ira! Where is your head, son? I thought you were out here chopping firewood and you're just daydreaming." Mama startled Ira back to reality. He had been haunted by the last conversation he had with Mattie before he left Kentucky. Now all he could think about was the desperation in her eyes.

"Sorry, Mama. I've just got some things weighing heavy on my mind. I'll get it done." Ira proceeded to return his focus to the woodpile.

"Alright, then. Supper will be ready soon." She walked away wondering what could be troubling her son. He had never acted this way. She suspected a woman was involved. "Good lord, I hope so," she muttered to herself.

Ira sat in front of the fireplace as his father strummed on the banjo. Rocking back and forth he would hum along to the familiar tunes. As much as he enjoyed his daddy's playing, he could not take his mind off of Mattie Akers. "Pa, I think I may head back to Kentucky a little early. Uncle Roy will probably be needing some help...with the holidays and all. You know, getting restocked and such." Ira hated working in the store. He would much rather be farming but he did not want his parents to know about his plan to help Mattie. But more importantly, that he was in love with a married woman.

"I'm surprised you enjoy the store so much." Pa said as he tuned his banjo, "I half expected you to not go back after Christmas. But if that's what you want, I'm sure Roy would appreciate it."

"It's not so much that I like it. It's just that I have committed myself to help out and learning the business. Uncle Roy is getting older and needs some help. I don't mind it too much."

"Well, you do what you feel is right. You're a man now, Ira. If you don't want to take over the store though, you need to be honest. You have brothers who could do it, too. Your Aunt Cora has some boys that might be interested as well. Just keep that in mind." He began playing
"It Came Upon a Midnight Clear." as the fire continued to glow.

"Thank you, Pa. I will. I think I'll leave early on the 26th before the New Year...help him get things closed out in the books." The two sat together in the warmth of the embers humming and playing until late into the night.

Rondal Gross could not sleep. His home felt like a tomb without his beloved Blue. The sight of Bob Akers sitting in the courtroom after the verdict was read haunted him and would continue to do so for many nights to come. As night turned into morning, his hatred for Berl Adams grew.

Christmas morning Mattie and her family gathered to go to church service. Mattie got through it in a daze. She smiled and returned greetings by those in attendance, but her mind was on Billy. Time was running out. She caught sight of Mr. Hobbs as they filed out after services. She purposely slowed down so that she could inquire about Ira's return.

"Merry Christmas, Mr. Hobbs. How are you this morning?"

"Merry Christmas to you, Mrs. Mattie. I'm very good thank you, very good indeed."

"So glad to hear it. I guess it's back to work for you tomorrow."

"Yes, ma'am. I will be closing out my books for the year this week. I'll be glad when Ira gets back. I'd like to show him the bookkeeping side of storekeeping."

"I see. Sounds like you will be busy this week. When do you expect him back?" Mattie tried to hide her anxiousness as she awaited his answer.

"Not till after the first of the year. He's visiting family, you know. I'll go over it with him when he gets back, but it's not the same."

"Yes, I'm sure you're right." Mattie's heart fell at the thought of waiting another week. "Mama and I will be by soon. Have a very Merry Christmas, Mr. Hobbs. And a Happy New Year!"

"And you as well, Mrs. Mattie! Thank you so much." Mr. Hobbs smiled having no idea the pain in Mattie's heart.

As her family gathered for dinner, Mattie went through the motions of preparation. She listened to the older generation reminisce of younger days. No one asked her about Billy. No one ever asked her. Everyone seemed content allowing him to be forgotten, pretending he no longer existed. Mattie spent the night weeping into her pillow. The world felt so heavy.

# CHAPTER 29

"I will be traveling to Owsley County to inform your wife of the verdict, Billy. Would you like me to deliver a message for her?"

"Sheriff, I would like to write her a letter and tell her myself if you don't mind. Instead of telling her, would you deliver the letter to Mr. Hobbs at the store? Her daddy won't let you near her. I would rather she hear it from me."

"You're probably right. Get the letter written and I will ride up there tomorrow. I sure hate all this, Billy. I really do."

"So do I, sheriff." Billy began writing his last words to Mattie.

*December 22, 1849*

*My Dearest Matilda,*

*As I write this to you, my greatest wish is that you know that my soul is at peace. God and justice have made their decision. The jury has found me guilty. Although we both know I am innocent and the true lawbreaker is gone from this world, I will accept my fate. I will join my sweet mother in Heaven on December 30th at noon. I know you will find it hard to understand and accept. God's ways are not our ways. I am choosing not to question my fate, but instead, to accept it and know he has a plan. Oh, how I will miss you, my love. I will miss raising our child. I wanted so badly to have a family with you. To teach our children how to farm and hunt. To pass on our love for these woods we call home. Stay strong, Mattie. Do not mourn for me for long. My hope for you and our little one is that you can live long and happy lives.*

*I love you. I love you.*

*Your loving husband,*

*Billy*

    Billy folded the letter and gave it to Sheriff Lawson without saying a word. He didn't have to, the air was heavy with the gravity of his fate.
    "I will deliver it tomorrow for you, Billy."
    "Much obliged, sheriff. Merry Christmas to you."
    The words stung Joe. He nodded sadly, "Thank you, Billy."
    Billy turned to see the snowflakes falling softly outside his window. Laying down on his cot, he fell quickly into a dreamless sleep.

# CHAPTER 30

Ira arrived at the store in the late afternoon hours of December 26th. Mr. Hobbs was surprised to see him.

"I wasn't expecting you back till after the first of the year!"

"I came back early. I figured you needed some help while you got the books in order." He couldn't tell his uncle about his plans to help Matilda Akers leave town.

"Wonderful! That will help me a bunch. To be honest, I wasn't sure if you'd be back. Doesn't seem like storekeeping is your thing."

"It's alright. I'd rather have a farm, but storekeeping is an honest living. I need to make sure I give it a fair shake."

Mr. Hobbs nodded his head in agreement and smiled. He was pleased with his nephew. Even if he chose to be a farmer, he was willing to keep trying.

"I'm glad you're back, Ira. I will start working on closing everything out for the year in the morning and you can run the store. Not much new. There's some mail behind the counter. A letter for Mrs. Jameson and one for Matilda Akers. If they come in, be sure that they get them."

"Yes, sir. I will. I'm going to go get settled and give Buck some water and a rest. I'll be in bright and early tomorrow."

"Fine, fine, I'll be done soon and we can have some supper. Ms. Thelma brought me over some food from their Christmas dinner. There should be enough for both of us to enjoy."

Thank you, uncle. That sounds good." Ira walked out and began leading Buck to the barn to rest. Buck had another big job coming up soon; he would need it.

Matilda woke up with one goal in mind, getting to town

to see if there was any word from Billy. She had not been able to sleep the night before due to her worry. The isolation and lack of information were driving her mad. Surely nothing would happen before the first of the year.

"Mama, don't you think we should go to the store for some dry goods?"

"I'll be going to the store in a couple of weeks. I don't need anything now, Matilda."

"We had a lot of company at Christmas, Mama. I'm sure you need to restock."

"I know what I have, Matilda. My goodness, you seem persistent about going to town. What's going on with you?"

Matilda decided to be honest. "Mama, I need to see if there is any word from Billy. The trial hasn't been going very good and…I just really need to know if there is any news."

Mama scowled. She didn't like to be reminded of Billy Akers. She also felt that her husband's tactics for handling the situation weren't right either. "I'll get the cart ready and go. I'll come up with something to tell your daddy and get him to hitch Tucker up before he goes hunting. Hopefully, he won't ask too many questions since he needs to get out to the woods."

Mattie hugged her mother tight and helped clean up the kitchen while she went to talk to her daddy. This had to work.

Soon Mama came back and told her to get ready, Daddy was hitching the trailer. "I didn't have to lie; he didn't ask a thing. He must be in a hurry this morning!" They loaded up in the wagon. Mama clucked to Tucker as they started toward Mr. Hobbs's store.

Ira was sweeping snow off of the steps of the store when he heard the sound of a wagon approaching. His heart jumped as he saw Mrs. Abner and Matilda Akers riding into town. He tried to hide both his excitement and nervousness about his promise made to Mattie. He smiled as they got closer.

"Good morning, ladies! I hope you had a nice holiday."

"Yes, Ira, it was lovely. Thank you." Mrs. Abner allowed Ira to help her down from the wagon. "And how was your Christmas? You spent it in Virginia, right? I'm actually a bit surprised to see you back so soon."

"Yes, ma'am. It was nice to visit. I came back early to help out Uncle Roy, lots to do to close up the year, you know."

"I imagine so. I'm going to go inside and pick up a few things. Come along Mattie, we'll check the mail."

"Mrs. Mattie, you did receive a letter. I will get it for you. It's behind the counter."

Mattie could feel her heart racing. "Thank you, Ira."

As Mama found herself caught up in conversation with Mr. Hobbs, Mattie went directly to the counter to retrieve her letter. She lowered her voice as she asked Ira, "Did you bring Buck back?"

"Yes, he's in the stable," Ira whispered back cautiously, "How are we going to do this Mrs. Mattie?"

Mattie made sure her mother was unaware of her conversation with Ira. "The day after tomorrow, Daddy is going hunting. He will be gone all night. I will sneak out just before dawn and meet you in front of the Spencer farm. Do you know where that is? There is a barn near the road, that's where I will be. Can you do that for me, Ira?" She waited anxiously for his reply as Mama and Mr. Hobbs rattled on about their family traditions over the holidays.

Ira looked Mattie in the eyes. They had never looked as green as they did at that moment. The world stopped. He seemed to forget to breathe. "Yes, Mrs. Mattie. I will do it...for you."

Mattie smiled and touched his hand. Ira felt his face flush. "Thank you, Ira. Thank you so much." She placed the letter in her dress and waited for Mama to finish her conversation. Mama turned and saw Mattie waiting.

"Oh, are we ready, Mattie?"

"Yes ma'am. I didn't mean to interrupt your conversation with Mr. Hobbs."

"Oh, no worries, Mrs. Mattie. We were just reminiscing. You ladies have a nice day now."

"Thank you, Mr. Hobbs. We'll be back next month for supplies." As Mama stepped out the door, Mattie knew she had no intention of returning next month.

"Make sure your daddy doesn't see that letter." Mama's gaze never left the road ahead.

Arriving home, Mama allowed Tucker to graze and went into the house. Mattie took her letter to a private spot in the wooded area beside the house. As she read, she allowed the tree to hold her body upright. The more she read, the weaker she became. Her body sank into the cold ground in a heap of sobs.

# CHAPTER 31

Berl Adams was busy preparing for his trip to Lexington. He wanted to get out of town before Billy was scheduled to hang. Bob Akers had left him feeling vulnerable with the Akers clan. There was no doubt that some would want revenge. Berl, his wife, and son would be leaving at daylight tomorrow. There was no time to waste. As he began to load their things in the wagon a shot rang out and a warm sensation hit his leg, taking him to the ground. He reached behind his thigh and felt the warm blood flowing from the fresh gunshot wound. Berl looked in disbelief at his bloody hand. Another shot rang out knocking him on his back. He reached for his shoulder feeling the fresh flow of blood. "Who are you??" Berl yelled at the trees above him. "Don't shoot! I'm unarmed!" Berl felt helpless as he lay on the ground bleeding.

"Bob Akers! Is that you?? Don't shoot me, Bob! It was nothing personal...Billy seemed guilty. Surely you see that. I have a son, too. I know it's hard to watch them die. Mine is slipping away, Bob! Please, don't kill me." Berl was near tears. No one answered him. The door flung open and his wife ran out.

"Berl! What is going on?" She knelt beside her husband. Blood covered his leg and upper right arm. "Let's get inside." She helped her husband up allowing him to put his weight on her. He limped slowly up the steps into the house, dragging his injured leg behind him.

As the door shut behind them, a lone figure watched from behind a rock several yards away. He uncocked his gun and relaxed his aim. Gathering his things, Rondal Gross prepared for his walk home. Before leaving his spot he looked down at the Adams home place.

"That was for Blue."

He grabbed his gun. A small hound dog followed behind him, a pup no more than three months old. "C'mon, Lady, let's go home." The pair trekked through the woods heading home.

Matilda sat on the cold ground for a long time. She had to pull herself together and face her parents without letting them know what was happening. If they became aware of Billy's fate, they would make it impossible for her to escape. Her life seemed to be built on lies.

"So? How is Billy?" Mama asked casually. Matilda had been burying her anger for so long. She couldn't wait to flee this prison.

"Everything is about the same," she lied, "the trial isn't going too well, though. The evidence is stacked against him." She hoped that Mama did not notice the puffiness in her eyes or the desperation in her voice.

"I'm sure it will all work out, Matilda," Mama said this almost in passing as she began dinner preparations. She had bought Mattie's lie or, at the very least, denied the knowledge of it.

"I hope you're right, Mama. Do you need help with anything? I'm going to go lay down for a little bit."

"No, I'm fine. Are you sick?"

"No, ma'am. I didn't sleep well last night. I just need a little rest if that's ok."

"Ok," Mama looked concerned, "I'll come get you when dinner is ready."

"Thank you, Mama." Mattie went to lay down, placing the letter under her pillow. Dawn was still several hours away and time was running out.

Ira was struggling to stay focused. He was nervous about what could happen to Mattie. A trip to Clay County on horseback wasn't easy. Add to it being a woman and unfamiliar with the horse and you have a potentially dangerous situation. If something happened to her, he would never forgive himself. If he backed out, Matilda would never forgive him. Ira could not stand the thought of that. He had to believe that she knew what she was doing. It was in Ira's best interest to accept the fact that Mattie belonged to another man and that man needed her; he needed to come to terms with that. But in the quiet of his days, all Ira could think about were those green eyes. Ira was picturing just that as he swept the store floor when Mr. Hobbs walked up behind him.

"Ira, I need you to help me with some of these counts…"

Ira jumped and called out, dropping his broom.

"My goodness, you are jumpy! You ok, Ira?"

"I'm sorry. Yes, uncle, I'm fine. Just daydreaming I guess. I didn't hear you walk up. I'll help you with the counts, of course." Ira was relieved by the distraction.

# CHAPTER 32

Matilda lay staring at the ceiling. Adrenaline was pumping through her veins. She envisioned every aspect of her trip. She would have to make stops for the horse to rest and drink. There was no time to waste, everything hinged on her arriving in Clay County before noon. After that, it would be too late.

Daddy was gone on his hunting trip. Mattie could hear her mother sleeping deeply in the next room. Mama was a heavy sleeper, but Mattie would have to be as quiet as possible to get out of the house. Unlike her father, mama could not outrun Mattie. As soon as she could see that dawn was breaking, Mattie slowly rose up and sat on the edge of the bed. She had hidden her dress under her blankets. Slowly and quietly she began changing. She had memorized every creak that the floorboards made and knew exactly which ones to avoid. The anticipation was overwhelming. She wanted to bolt out the door and down the road toward freedom, but she didn't dare. Patience was the key to saving Billy. Step by careful step she eased out of her room and through the kitchen toward the door. Her bare feet carefully chose their landing while Mama's slow steady breathing assured Mattie that she was completely unaware of her escape. Slowly lifting the wood latch on the door, she opened it only as far as she needed to slide through. A small creak came from the hinges. Mattie stopped and listened for her mother. Mama's breathing did not waver. She continued to slumber as Mattie slowly closed the door behind her. Carefully choosing each step, she quietly descended from the porch. Resisting the urge to run, she walked across the property until she reached the road. She bent down to put her shoes on her feet and began walking down the road toward the meeting spot. After only a few steps, Mattie broke into a run.

Running down the dirt road, Mattie dared not turn around in fear that her father would be right behind her. As she found herself getting further from her parents' home, tears began falling down her cheeks. All of the feelings of hopelessness were being replaced with determination. She arrived at their meeting place. Ira wasn't there. What if he changed his mind? What if he didn't show? Everything hinged on him providing the horse and the clock was ticking. Pacing nervously, she went over the route in her head. If she kept a steady pace, she should arrive before noon. She had to, Billy's life depended on it. Where the hell was Ira?! Mattie's anxiety was increasing.

"If he doesn't show, I'll run to Clay County," she whispered to herself.

The sound of movement could be heard to her left. Mattie hid in the bushes and listened intently. The familiar sound of hoof beats was coming down the road. Please, for the love of God, be Ira. As the sounds became clearer, she could hear that the horse was being walked, not ridden. As they came to the site of the barn. The sounds stopped.

"Woah, Buck, we'll wait right here."

"Ira? Is that you?" Mattie whispered.

"It's me, Mattie. Where are you?"

Mattie came out from behind the bushes. "I was hiding. I wanted to make sure it wasn't anyone else."

"Sorry, it took me a while. I was afraid to make too much noise, even in the barn. I was scared to death that I would wake up Uncle Roy. Here is Buck. He's a fast gallop, but be sure to rest him. He's gentle but can be skittish sometimes. Are you sure you know what you are doing, Mattie? This is going to be dangerous out there by yourself."

"I know what I'm doing. It's a long story, Ira, but I have no choice. I have to do this."

Ira handed Mattie the reins. He patted Buck on the neck. "Behave yourself with Mrs. Mattie now." He turned to Mattie.

Mattie could barely see his features in the moonlight, but she could see and sense his concern.

"Please be careful. I hope you can do what you need to. I'll see you when you get back."

"Thank you, Ira. Thank you so much for this. I'll be back in a few days. Buck is in good hands, I promise."

"I'm more worried about you, Mattie," he stopped himself from saying more, "just be careful, ok?"

"I will." Mattie put her foot in the stirrup and mounted her horse. She started down the road in the direction of town. Mattie needed to get out before anyone saw her.

"I'm coming, Billy."

# CHAPTER 33

Billy hadn't slept. This would be his last day on Earth. It all went so fast. He only wished that he could see Matilda once more. Had he only listened to his wife's fear and discomfort with Frank Prewitt, none of this would have happened. Billy took comfort in the fact that Frank Prewitt was dead and could no longer hurt anyone else. Maybe that was God's purpose, to get rid of that son of a bitch, Prewitt. Mattie would be protected from the judgment of the town for what happened that night. It had never crossed Billy's mind until now, just how unfair it was for women who have been raped by a man. Mattie fought for her life, for the life of their baby. The evidence was all over the floors and walls of their home. The only one at fault was Frank and he deserved what he got and Mattie deserved to live in peace. If that meant sacrificing himself, so be it.

He closed his eyes and tried to picture her face, her smile, the softness in her eyes. Billy recalled scenes from their life. The first time he saw her, the weekly meetings in the shade while her mama picked up supplies, their wedding day...everything felt like a distant memory, a lifetime ago.

The sun rose outside his window. The colors glowed pink and purple across the sky. He watched intently, unlike any other sunset he had seen. He wondered if there were sunsets in Heaven. Could it be more glorious than this? Tomorrow he may be watching it with Jesus. It was surreal. Sheriff Lawson walked in with a plate.

"Hey, Billy. You wouldn't tell me what you wanted yesterday so I just brought you a big breakfast. You always seem to enjoy breakfast."

Sheriff Lawson hadn't been able to choke down anything that morning. He was sick about the day's activities. Today would stand out as the lowest point of his career.

"You can set it down, sheriff. I'm not very hungry but I may take a few bites."

Sheriff Lawson set the plate inside the cell and left Billy to be alone with his thoughts. He walked across the road to check on Marcus. As a mortician, Marcus had the unfortunate job of also holding the position of executioner. It was a position he hated but took seriously. Joe wanted to check in on him and see how he was doing. Like Joe, Marcus was fond of Billy. This was going to be a difficult day for everyone.

Bob Akers had been awake for hours. As soon as the sun began to rise, he began his walk to his beloved Sarah's, grave. Although she would not be able to reply, she was the only person who would understand; she was the only one he could talk to. As he approached the tombstone underneath the big poplar tree, he removed his hat. Stopping at the foot of her grave, he felt a lump in his throat.

"Hey, Sarah. I sure do miss you. I think about you every day...especially when I'm cookin'. I just can't cook like you did. I'm tryin' though. As lonely as it gets down here, I'm glad you're not here to see this. It looks like your boy is coming up to join you. It's not fair, Sarah. Justice isn't always fair, I guess. No doubt in my mind he was framed and I think I know who and how, but I can't prove it. It's a shame. He's a good boy, a kind man. He's not like me. I'm proud of him, though. He has shown such loyalty and courage to protect Matilda. She hasn't been around. I'm not even sure she knows. Billy says that her parents are protecting her...sounds like controlling her if you ask me. But nobody is asking me, are they, Sarah? If I were being honest, I don't want to go today, but I have to. I have to be there for Billy. I have to say goodbye to our son. And you're about to say hello. I reckon I will bury him right here next to you. I'm tired of goodbyes, darlin'. I'm not sure if you can see me, but if you can, I need you today. I love you, Sarah. I miss you." Bob placed his hat back on his head and began his trip toward the inevitable.

Marcus sat quietly in his office doing paperwork when Joe entered. "Hello, sheriff. I'd say good morning but it certainly would feel like a lie."

Joe sat down, letting out a long sigh. "You are certainly right about that, Marcus. I keep wondering if there is something I missed. Of all the men in this town, Billy is the last one I would have ever expected to be in this position. What do you think Marcus? Did I miss something?"

"Not that I can see. I looked at the same evidence you did. I think for me it's a matter of motive. I can't imagine he would kill Frank in cold blood. The evidence says that either he or Matilda killed him, but why? With neither of them talking, there's very little we can do to help him. We can only conclude what the evidence presents." Marcus shrugged his shoulders and shook his head. "It's a shame, though, a crying shame."

Both men sat in silence, taking in the gravity of the day to come.

Mama stared into Mattie's empty room. She had heard her daughter sneaking out. She knew where she was going. Pretending to sleep, she did not attempt to stop her. She was not sure how Mattie planned on getting to Billy, but she was sure that whatever the plan was, it was well thought out. There was no need in trying to stop her. Mama knew that if she were in her shoes, she would do the same thing. George would be infuriated. He would have to accept it. Right was right and wrong was wrong. She would settle for saying a prayer for Mattie's safety and the sparing of Billy's life.

Mattie was trying to keep a steady pace. She was careful not to push Buck too far for fear of him giving out. She wanted to run him as hard as she could until they got to Clay County, but that would be foolish. Looking into the sky gave her pause as the sun's placement was telling her it was near or around 9 a.m. She had to arrive before noon if she wanted to save Billy. She stopped by a creek and dismounted.

As Buck drank from the creek, Mattie gently stroked his

neck and shoulders. She would need to run him hard to get to Billy in time. Memories flashed in her mind like still-frame pictures. The first time their eyes met. Their wedding day without the support of their parents. Their life together had been so simple and perfect. They were so happy. Mattie shook off memories of that fateful night with Frank Prewitt. How could one person have the power to destroy so many lives? She allowed Buck to graze for just a few minutes more.

"It's time to go, Buck. Time is slipping away." She mounted the horse and continued her journey.

Billy sat silently in his cell. He tried to pray, but he had nothing to say. There were no more words that hadn't already been spoken. Emotionless, he sat looking straight ahead, awaiting his fate. Bob Akers walked into the jail for one last visit with his son.

"Hey, Billy. How are you doin'?"

"As well as could be expected, I guess."

Bob nodded his head in understanding. "I visited your mother this mornin'. She'll be waiting for you. I'm not sure how that makes you feel, but I'm hopin' it brings you comfort."

Billy felt a knot forming in his throat. He swallowed hard, he did not want to break down in front of his daddy. He needed to stay strong. "It does. I appreciate it, Daddy. I look forward to seeing her." Billy swallowed hard again. "I'm sorry. I'm sorry to put you through this."

"No. Don't you dare apologize! I hate that I am losing you, but you have given up your life to protect someone you love. That's a noble act. I'm proud of you, son. You are stronger than I ever gave you credit for. This is an injustice. You shouldn't be losing your life today. Those damn Caudills are to blame...and they will pay. But I'm proud of how you have faced this."

Billy nodded, making eye contact with his father. It was the first time he had heard him say that he was proud of him. "Thank you, sir. I appreciate that." He paused for a moment. "I love you, Daddy."

Bob had never been one to say I love you, except to Sarah.

But this circumstance was different. "I love you, too, son."

"Please promise me you will let Mattie know that I love her...and the baby."

"I will."

Bob turned and left. All that needed to be said had been said. It was now time to face the day. He passed Joe as he was leaving.

"Sheriff."

"Bob."

Greetings were kept simple but respectful. Bob knew that the sheriff, too, was a victim to the dishonest ways of the Caudill clan. He held no grudge. Sheriff Lawson dared not disrespect the somberness of the day with any form of pleasantness. Joe grabbed his keys and proceeded to unlock the cell door.

"You have one more visitor, Billy."

# CHAPTER 34

Mattie had been running at a slow but steady gallop for the last couple of hours. By her calculations, she was still over an hour away. She looked at the sky, the day had been cold and cloudy, but she could see the sun was getting high. She was running out of time.

"Buck it's time. Let's go!"

Mattie kicked Buck in the side hard. "Hyah!" Buck roared into a full gallop. The cold wind blew back Mattie's hat, her hair flowing wildly. The hoof beats hit the cold ground, steady and true. Mattie leaned forward, her eyes fully focused on the path before her.

"I'm coming, my love."

Sheriff Lawson opened the cell door and allowed the preacher, Brother Lewis Mitchell, to enter. "Brother Lewis will spend a few minutes with you and then we will get you ready." Joe closed the cell door behind the reverend and stepped away. He was struggling with the performance of today's duties.

"Hello, son. I wanted to say a prayer for you before they take you out. Before we do that, if there are any unforgiven sins that you would like to talk about, or any pain that you would like to get off of your chest, now is the time. What can I do for you today, Billy?"

"I appreciate that, pastor. I'm sure there are things I have done that God isn't happy with me about. I've tried my best and that's all I can say about that. The only pain I feel currently is that I have to leave my family. That's mighty hard. But a prayer would be nice. Thank you, sir."

Brother Lewis sat quietly listening to the young man. "I'm

sure this is all very difficult for you, leaving your family, facing death. But, and I say this as a man of God and your friend, Billy, confessing and letting go of the reason that you are here today will certainly bode well for you when you meet the Father." His gaze rested gently on Billy. Billy met his gaze without wavering.

"I am only guilty of being an Akers, pastor. Nothing more."

"I see." The preacher was visibly shaken. "Shall we pray for your soul as it enters Heaven today?"

"Yes, please." Billy bowed his head and closed his eyes.

Brother Lewis watched the prayerful prisoner curiously. Could it be that an innocent man was dying today? Shaken, he led them in prayer asking for a painless demise with acceptance into the Kingdom before the day was through.

"Amen."

Billy raised his head and smiled kindly to the preacher. "Amen."

"May God have mercy on your soul, Billy." Upon hearing his own words, Brother Lewis added. "May God have mercy on ours as well."

He called to the sheriff to open the door. As he and Joe stepped outside the jail into the cold morning, the pastor turned to the sheriff.

"I hope you are right, sheriff. I suspect an innocent man is dying today."

Sheriff Lawson felt his heart skip. He did not want his own doubts to show. "He was judged by a jury of his peers, pastor. Not me."

Brother Lewis said no more, he just turned and walked toward the church. He needed some time with the Lord himself.

Mattie was making good time. Buck had proved to be all that Ira had promised. At this pace, they should arrive in Clay County in time. It was then that Mattie sensed a change in Buck's gait. He was slowing down. She kicked his side. "Hyah!" But he continued to slow his pace. He did not slow to a walk, but he was now at a trot.

"No! No! This can't be happening!" Mattie felt the panic in her rise.

"Woah." Buck slowed and came to a stop. Mattie dismounted to check for leg injuries. Running her arms down each leg, nothing felt odd. She gently lifted the leg to examine the hoof. They were completely impacted by dirt. She would have to clean them out to ensure there were no rocks or debris present that would make running uncomfortable. She tried clearing the packed dirt with her fingers but she was struggling to make headway. Letting go of the leg, she began walking the area in search of something to use as a tool to clean his hooves. Lacking sticks that would be strong enough, she searched for rocks with sharp edges. Desperation was overwhelming her. She stopped in the middle of the open field, Buck grazing close by, and took a deep breath.

"Stop. You mustn't panic. Lord, if you hear my prayers, please God, PLEASE, show me a rock."

Calming her nerves, she began methodically surveying the ground, occasionally picking up rocks that were too smooth to help her. Tears began to well up in her eyes and stream down her cheeks. With her face resting in her palms, she stood in the cold, alone, and cried. Defiance came over her like a hot wave as she looked up to the Heavens.

"One damn rock is all I am asking for! Just one!"

Her shoulders dropped and a feeling of hopelessness was about to take hold when she saw a hint of gray among the grass. Quickly, she fell to her knees to examine her find. A perfectly edged rock. She began lifting each hoof and cleaning out the packed dirt. If she did not find the culprit causing the issue, she might not be able to run him. As she dug out the dirt in the third hoof, a jagged rock was pressed deep within the center. She pulled it out and cleared out the area around it. Mattie knew this had to be the problem but she wanted to avoid any more interruptions. She cleaned out the fourth hoof. Keeping her newfound tool, she placed it in her saddlebag, mounted Buck, and kicked his ribs. "Hyah!" Buck tore into a full gallop. Rested from his break, his renewed energy was apparent in his speed. "Thank you, Jesus."

# CHAPTER 35

Sheriff Lawson led Billy to the town center. Billy kept his head high and gaze forward as he walked toward the gallows built specifically for this occasion. A large crowd surrounded the platform as Billy walked toward his fate. Side-eyed glances, whispering, laughing, and conversing, it was a feeling of celebration instead of an impending death. As he stepped up onto the center stage, he immediately saw in the front row, standing tall and strong, his father, Bob Akers. Marcus walked up the steps and stood to the right of him; the sheriff stood to the left. Judge Wilson spoke to the crowd.

"Citizens of Clay County, we are gathered here today to carry out the last act of justice in the case of Clay County vs William Akers. The Bible says an eye for an eye; thus the law says a life for a life. Let what you witness today be a warning, especially to those of you who have chosen to kill another simply by the name they carry. If you are found guilty of murder, no matter who you are, what position you hold, or how much money you carry...you will suffer this same fate."

Judge Wilson turned to face Billy. Billy looked him directly in the eyes. The judge did not falter.

"William Akers, you have been found guilty by a jury of your peers in the death of one Frank Prewitt and have been sentenced to be hanged until dead. Do you have any last words?"

"Yes, sir. I do."

Sheriff Lawson stepped behind Billy and joined Marcus on the other side. Marcus looked pale.

"I stand before you, an innocent man. I also stand before you, as an Akers. I do not have the money to purchase justice as the Caudills do and because of that, I will soon join my dear mother in Heaven and leave behind my..."

Bob Akers spoke up. "Not another word, son. Many a man has died for the love of a woman. Do not give them the privilege of your truth."

Billy looked at his father and nodded knowingly. He looked to Marcus who was visibly shaken.

"Do what you need to do. I have no more to say."

Marcus stepped forward and proceeded to place the noose around Billy's neck.

Mattie's face was numb against the cold air as she and Buck galloped through the pasture. The nostrils of the horse were flaring as his breath blew out like smoke in the winter temperatures. Mattie looked at the sky. The sun was almost directly above her. If she continued in this direction she would never make it in time. There was a shortcut through the woods that would lead her to Coomer Ridge. The terrain was dangerous but it would take her to a lookout point directly above town. She had no choice. She pulled the reins to the right, running Buck through the woods toward the ridge.

"I'm coming, Billy."

With intense focus, Matilda led her horse through the trees and brush. One wrong decision could mean death for them both. Low-hanging branches slapped her face. She could feel the blood trickling down her cheeks and chin. Coming around the bend, Mattie noticed the terrain ahead looked different. She had forgotten about Spruce Gap. The gap at the top of the ridge was about ten-feet-wide, the drop, however, was 100 feet or more. They were too close to slow down and there was no time to lose. Buck would have to jump. Matilda kicked him hard in the side so that he would not slow down. "Hyuh!" Buck neighed loudly but never hesitated and leaped over the gap. They were almost to Coomer Ridge. The ledge was in the distance.

"Woah, Buck!"

She quickly dismounted Buck and ran for the ledge. Buck would not be able to make the steep trail. The ledge offered the perfect view of the town. A large crowd was gathered around a stage. But, it wasn't a stage, it was the gallows and Billy stood there while a man placed a noose around his neck.

"No!"

Billy felt the stiff rope rest along his neck and back. A sackcloth was placed over his head. He felt no fear. Closing his eyes he pictured Mattie. Remembering the look in her eyes the first time they met. A smile found its way to his lips. He did not hear Marcus next to him.

"May God have mercy on your soul."

Marcus stepped back and released the trap door. Billy's neck snapped immediately as he was immersed into the darkness of death. As he dangled from the rope, Sheriff Lawson wiped away tears with his handkerchief. The crowd roared in a mix of shock, horror, and celebration. Bob closed his eyes and stood motionless. And in all the chaos and excitement, no one heard the screams and shrieks coming from the top of Coomer Ridge as Mattie crumpled to the ground.

※ ※ ※

Matilda lay in the bed, weak from reliving the memories. She looked at Ira who sat looking at her in disbelief.

"When I came back, I told you that I couldn't make it in time. You knew my husband had been hung, but you didn't know the reason why. You never asked, because you are a gentleman and respected my grief. I never told you, because I was ashamed. I never forgave Mama and Daddy for holding me hostage. I still don't. But I need to confess before I meet my maker. I am the one who killed Frank Prewitt, not Billy. I have no regrets for killing him. I only regret not speaking up for myself and saving Billy. You are a kind man, Ira. I grew to love you. I love our children and will miss them. I will miss you. But it is time for me to join Billy. This is both my reward and punishment."

Mattie closed her eyes. Ira stood next to her observing

her frail body barely breathing. He leaned down and kissed her forehead.

"I will always love you. You are the most beautiful woman I have ever seen. You have been through so much. I know you need to go, I understand."

He gathered the children to come and tell their mother that they loved her as she slowly slipped away. Before night fell, she was gone.

Sheriff Lawson heard of Matilda's death. The news awakened the uncertainties he had felt about the death of Frank Prewitt and the hanging of Billy Akers. He could not shake the thoughts from his mind. To clear his head, he decided to take a ride up to the Akers farm. It had sat abandoned since the trial ten years ago. Not much was happening around town, so he mounted his horse and began following the familiar trail where it all began.

# CHAPTER 36

Mattie walked down a trail into a clearing. All of her life she had been told about pearly gates and streets of gold, but this looked more like home. She stepped out and looked around. She felt no pain. Her body was completely restored. She looked around and saw the home that she and Billy had built.

"I'm home! I don't understand."

She walked closer to the house. The air was warm and smelled of honeysuckle. Standing in front of the cabin, she could not believe her eyes.

"Is this Heaven?"

"Not yet."

She turned quickly in the direction of the voice. There, by the workshop, stood Billy holding the hand of a small child.

"Oh my goodness!" Mattie clasped her hands over her mouth in shock. Billy let go of the child's hand. A little boy ran toward her gleefully.

"Mommy!"

Mattie bent down and picked him up hugging him and smothering him with kisses. Billy walked toward her.

'Billy? Is that really you?"

"It is. We've been waiting for you." He leaned in and kissed her forehead. Mattie felt pure joy which was soon followed by guilt.

"Billy...I lied to you...our second baby...I thought I was pregnant but when I found out I wasn't, I was afraid..."

"Shhhhh...I know, I know. It's ok. I understand."

Mattie smiled. "I missed you so."

Billy smiled back. "I know. We're together now.' The moment was interrupted by the sound of hoof beats approaching. They both turned to see Joe riding up.

"Who is that, Mommy?"

"That's the sheriff, baby."

Joe let Bullet graze while he took a look around. The place was overgrown and empty. Bob Akers had taken the animals back to his farm, but no one had the heart to sell the place. It just sat here, frozen in time.

The door to Billy's workshop sat slightly ajar. He remembered the cradle and small toys he had found years earlier when investigating. Stepping inside, he wondered if any of those things were left behind. The shed was empty. Bob must have cleaned them out. As Joe was walking out, a board moved beneath his feet. He looked down and saw something between the floorboards. The board lifted easily showing a secret compartment.

"How clever!" Joe would have never found it were it not for the leaking roof that warped the wood.

Inside were hand-carved animals. Joe was sure they were toys carved by Billy. He caught sight of a small book. Removing it, he opened to the first page. It was a journal! After reading the first couple of pages he realized...this was the journal of Matilda Akers!

Sheriff Lawson stepped out and sat on the stoop to investigate his find.

"My journal!" Mattie was panicked.

"It'll be ok." Billy consoled her.

Joe began reading every page.

*December 10, 1864*

*Billy is going hunting tomorrow. I wish I could go with him but he is afraid for me to be out in my condition. My belly is growing and this makes me excited. I can't wait for the baby to get here. I will have to take out my dresses to make more room. Billy has said that Frank Prewitt will be coming over tomorrow. I wish he wasn't, I do not like the way he looks at me. He gives me a bad feeling. Billy thinks I worry too much, maybe he is right. I will try to busy myself with my sewing while he is here.*

*December 15, 1864*
*The baby is gone. I can hardly bear it.*

*December 18, 1864*
*I have found it hard to write about this but I feel it might help me. Frank Prewitt killed our baby. I still can't remember everything as I almost died myself. Billy said Frank is gone but he won't tell me where. The things he did to me were awful. How can Billy ever look at me the same way?*

*December 20, 1864*
*I remember everything. I killed Frank Prewitt. I had to or he would have killed me. The sheriff came by today to ask Billy some questions. They found his body on our farm. My sweet Billy buried him to protect me. I want to tell the sheriff what happened, but Billy won't let me. I'm so scared.*

He slowly closed the journal, wiping his face with his hands. His gut feeling had been right. Something had always been missing and that was the truth. The evidence had betrayed him. Joe sat quietly for a long time. He rose and went back inside the shed, placing the journal back where he found it. Shutting the door behind him, he looked up at the sky above.

"I'm sorry, Billy."

Billy smiled and looked at Mattie. "It's time for us to go."

Mattie looked confused. "Aren't we staying here?"

"No, Mattie. This isn't our home anymore. Follow me. I didn't want to go without you."

Taking her hand, the three of them turned and began walking into the forest. Sheriff Lawson looked up to see a family of cardinals chirping on a nearby branch. He hoped it was a good sign.

As Mattie, Billy, and their child walked toward their eternal home, Sheriff Lawson mounted Bullet and began to head back to town, his belief in justice forever changed.

# ACKNOWLEDGEMENT

My first debt of gratitude is to thank my wonderfully creative offspring, Lucas and Kenzie. You not only continuously inspire me with your own projects, you have never, not once, made me feel silly for mine.

Thank you so much Terri Crowe and Denise Gerkens for patiently proofreading every chapter. Terri did it twice, so double thank you, Terri.

Mama Carol King, aka "Coach." You have told me repeatedly, for years, to write. I finally listened. Thank you for believing in me.

The Clay County Historical Society who answered the call and recommended books to read that might help me to understand Matilda more deeply. You are so gracious.

To my "guinea pigs," Tracey, Cherylena, Kathy, Jeleana, Dee, Allison, and Sue. Thank you for being my friends and for your input.

Mom and Dad, thank you...just for being.

Michael, thank you for your support. You may never read it, but you encouraged me to write it.

# ABOUT THE AUTHOR

## Lisa R. Bush

Lisa is a writer living in Central Kentucky with her dogs, Maya and Daisy, and cats, Tiger and Pip. She is the mother of Lucas and Kenzie and great-great-granddaughter of Matilda Baker. This is her first published novel.

Made in the USA
Monee, IL
13 April 2022